MOTHER G(

RHYMES,

JINGLES.

,(MPLETE EDITION, WITH NOTES AND CRITICAL
ILLUSTRATIVE REMARKS

By W. GANNON.

NEW YORK:

HURST & COMPANY,

PUBLISHERS.

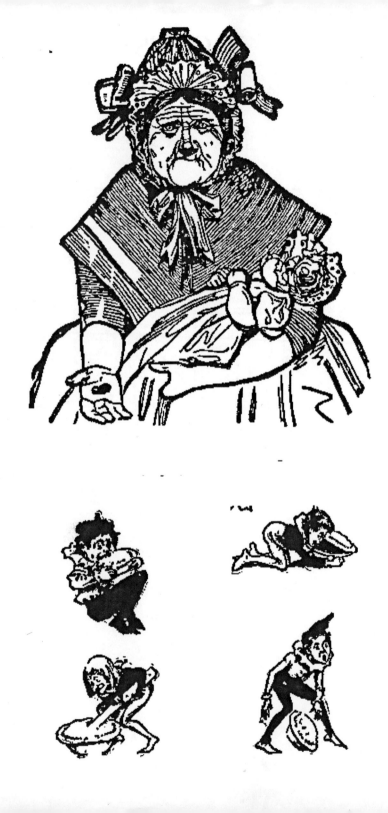

INTRODUCTION.

I.

FROM the vantage ground of fifty—that age when, forehanded, swift we
Round up treasure in a thrifty pile for possible future use,
We're called, in gen'rous spirit, to debit life's demerit,
And credit own to first inspirings of our now successful Muse—
To give and take with even hand—the gain is Truth's, e'en though we lose.

II.

Lose what! The lime-light glory, self-trained on "self-made" story,
That in the days of yore we set such monumental store by?
Though still fain we'd face the mirror where gleams the mirage of our lives,
"A saner, sad reflection," a wiser introspection,
An early recollection slants the shadow, and it gives!

III.

No architects of life are we! our forbears duly earned the fee
Of knowledge, life and liberty, so freely hurled adown the ages—
If haply we assimilate a maxim or a thought that's great,
And primp it to a fine estate, may we loll back and pose as sages?
Ask the publisher, who coldly looks upon our work as—pages.

IV.

And so the boy's the *pere* of man, ("since Adam delved and Eve
    span,")
And ere his Cupid's bow began its 'prenticeship to lisplngs,
His petaled ears and star-gemmed eyes had found a new and
    wondrous use
In drawing in the honeyed rhyme, the cymbal-sounding eerie
    chime
Of the " Once upon a time !" as told by Grand old Mother Goose.

V.

Ring the changes once again ! Let's hark back to Mother's
    strain !
Aside with pomp, with grime, with gain ! We call an honorable
    truce !
" Little Boy Blue, come blow your horn !" Rouse the echoes of
    our morn !
Appear ! thou " Maiden all Forlorn," " Old King Cole," " Wise
    Doctor Goose,"
" Simple Simon," " Little Bo-Peep," and " Priest all Shaven and
    Shorn !"

VI.

A thousand strings are thrummed—all good or ill in life is
    summed
Between those pictured leaves we thumbed in the days when
    time was nought—
Elfin cloudland, wraith of mistfield, peace of forest, rip of river,
In iridescent colors brushed, flecked with glow-worm gems en-
    crushed,
Live with us until life is hushed, and will live on and on forever !

VII.

Who's he can sum the honest dues her goslings owe in th' abstruse

For life-guide hints to Mother Goose—hints to fit or king or clown:

As—"One foot up, t'other down, *that's* the way to London town !"

So, self-help, plodding, gains the crown—a leaven ever fresh for use—

From childhood's *alma mater*—our charming second Mother —Goose!

JULY 25, 1902.

HISTORY OF MOTHER GOOSE.

TO "begin at the beginning" with this immortal classic of babyhood, we should probably have to go back to the Garden of Eden, for to Mother Love must be accorded the progressive authorship of "Mother Goose."

And the ways of motherhood are the same the wide world over —tender, watchful, vigilant—madly proud of the first physical essays that go to prove her bantling "the most wonderful ever" —keenly alert to catch and translate the earliest lispings of her darling—and prompt to fan into intelligence the first vital spark of infantine intellect.

It is certain that the Chaldean, Hebrew and Roman matrons crooned inspiring song and story into the infantile ears of prophets, kings and warriors, just as "my lady" of to-day breathes the story of "The House that Jack Built" or "The Death of Cock Robin" into the ears of future presidents, statesmen, painters and poets. Indeed, the framework of "The House that Jack Built" is Chaldean, as will be seen from the curious addenda attached to that story in the present volume.

Andrew Lang, who has devoted some of his valuable time toward the discovery of the authorship of "Mother Goose," asks: "Had we a 'Mother Goose' before Perrault's 'Mere l'Oye' became familiar here? Grimm says Perrault borrowed his title from 'a fabliau;' but this is vague, and Grimm may have had 'La Reine Pedauque' in his mind. We folk-lorists, who trace kin in the early way—through the mother's side—we goslings of Mother Goose—should know more about the ancestress of us all."—[*London Athenæum*, vol. for 1887, page 287.]

The title of the work referred to by Mr. Lang is usually translated, "Tales of my Mother Goose;" but it will be conceded that the rendering is somewhat free. The Frenchman, Charles Perrault, brought out this work—a collection of fairy tales – in the year 1697, his daughter's name, Perrault d'Armancourt, appearing on the title-page as author.

There is no interior resemblance between Perrault's book and our "Mother Goose," but the coincidence in title has served to excite remark as well as to provoke research.

"Mother Goose" is very English in its allusions, idioms and literary mannerisms, so much so that probably nine out of ten believe it had its origin in the land of Shakespeare and Milton. That the rhymes and stories were, in the main, imported, via folk-lore, there can be no manner of doubt—and that all the nations of the earth contributed to this grand mosaic is plainly evident—yet to our own great nation must be conceded the honor of first collecting and printing "Mother Goose's Melodies," substantially as we have them to-day.

Even to the title (notwithstanding the Perrault coincidence) the work is American, being named in compliment to a Boston lady, whose antecedents we have been enabled to follow so closely as to eliminate any possible doubt from the matter.

To William A. Wheeler, author of a "Dictionary of Noted Names of Fiction," are we indebted for the statement that "Mother Goose" was named for a real character, whose true name was Elizabeth Vergoose.

Vertigoose was the original family name of this good dame, when her ancestors reached these shores from England, in the year of 1650. This three-syllabled name was eventually clipped, as above stated, from whence the transition to one syllable— Goose—was familiarly simple. Under this name she had the happy chance to meet with one Thomas Fleet, an English disciple of "the art preservative," who reached the town of Boston in the early part of the eighteenth century, under cover of "seeking his fortune."

He found it—in marrying one of the numerous daughters of the good dame—supplementing this serious step by setting up a printing office on his own account, which apparently flourished from the start. It being a common thing in those days for printers to add a publishing department, as a side issue to their main business, the enterprising Fleet determined to enter the lists with his competitors. And here he probably found a congenial work-mate in his mother-in-law, whose large family presupposes the acquirement and use of an extensive repertory of child-satisfying story and verse, gleaned from her foregatherers, and, no doubt added to by herself, as she could easily pass for the typical "old woman who lived in a shoe," being the mother and stepmother of no less than sixteen children. At any rate, in the Year of Our Lord, 1719, there appeared from Fleet's press an unpretentious volume, entitled, "Songs for the Nursery, or, Mother Goose's Melodies for Children—printed by Thomas Fleet, at his printing house, Pudding Lane. Price, Two Coppers."

It may be well to state here that Pudding Lane has disappeared from the face of Boston's map, giving place to a less hearty but more euphonious designation—Devonshire street.

The record of marriages in the City Registrar's office of Boston shows that, on June 8, 1715, the Rev. Cotton Mather married Thomas Fleet to Elizabeth Goose. The happy couple took up their residence in Pudding Lane, under the same roof that covered the historic printing office.

All annals are silent as to the future efforts and history of the Fleets and the Gooses, save the stone annals of the churchyard, from which we gather that the last of the name of Goose died nearly a hundred years ago (in 1807,) and was laid to rest in the

Old Granary Burying Ground, "where probably the whole brood now repose."

Bowditch, in his book of "Suffolk Names," refers to "the wealthy family of Goose," and says they were extensive land-holders in Boston as early as 1660.

In order to present a full and impartial account of the origin of this work, we must not fail to insert here a recent statement made by an apparently well-informed correspondent of the *Boston Transcript*, who, while conceding that the Boston "Mother Goose" was the first collected edition of the famous "Melodies" put into print, yet says: "It is well-known to antiquarians that more than two hundred years ago there was a small book in circulation in London, bearing the name of 'Rhymes for the Nursery, or Lull-Bies for Children,' which contained many of the identical pieces which have been handed down to us under the 'Mother Goose' title."

Wheeler declares that our English cousins have had no acquaintance with any other "Mother Goose" than Perrault's and Dibdin's—no English bibliographical work consulted by him contains the name; "it is not mentioned in any catalogue of 'chap-books,' 'garlands,' popular histories, old or rare books, or the like."

Even Halliwell, in his "Nursery Rhymes of England," makes no mention of "Mother Goose."

Wheeler's reference to Dibdin needs explanation. The latter's work was a pantomime, which turned on the theme of "the goose that laid a golden egg," and which, of course, has no bearing on the present inquiry. Charles Dibdin, though remembered principally as a writer of sturdy sea-songs, was a comedian and playwright of great power, who, in the year 1806, produced this pantomime, under the name of "Mother Goose, or the Golden Egg." Strangely enough, through Charles

Dickens, in his "Life of Grimaldi," we learn that this pantomime was produced at Covent Garden, and had a run of ninety-two nights, "acquiring"—we use the words of Dickens—"a degree of popularity unprecedented in the history of pantomime." Later on, our own pantomimist, Fox, it will be recalled, borrowing his title, too, from "Mother Goose," played "Humpty Dumpty" by the year, successively! beating all playhouse records before or since.

Touching on the curious similarity of title between the French book of fairy tales and the American book of melodies, a French writer, named Collin de Planay, furnishes a strange historical narrative, explanatory of the naming of Perrault's book. The tale is thus condensed, and given without prejudice to religion or morals, solely for the purpose of throwing any side-light available on any and everything connected with the authorship, printing, and naming of "Mother Goose:"

King Robert II. of France took to wife his relative Bertha, but was at once commanded by Pope Gregory V. to relinquish her, and to perform a seven-years' penance for marrying within the forbidden degree of consanguinity. The King refused, and was promptly excommunicated. This action on the part of Rome placed the Kingdom interdict, and the royal family found itself forsaken by all, save two old retainers, who remained loyal, despite their threatened spiritual death. The hardships the royal pair endured during this first recorded example of "boycott," brought on premature confinement to the Queen, when her wily enemies contrived to foist upon the harassed King a featherless goose, horrifying him with the thought that his wife had given birth to it. And so he repented his sin, repudiated Bertha, and made his peace with Rome.

From this tale has sprung a proverbial French saying in reference to incredible or extravagant stories: that it must have happened "when Queen Bertha spun," and they call such a tale one of "Queen Goose's " or " Mother Goose's stories." This is said to be carried out to the letter in the first editions of Perrault's book, "where the front page pictures ' Mother Goose' at her distaff, and surrounded by a group of children, whom she holds entranced by her wondrous tales."

The writer has never had the good fortune to handle a copy of the first "Mother Goose"—the Thomas Fleet and Boston publication—but that it was fully in keeping with its "two coppers" price is well-known. The illustrations were startling attempts, and the cover picture is described as "something, probably intended to represent a goose, with a very long neck and a very wide open mouth."

But Thomas Fleet "builded better than he knew," and, despite the crude output from his modest press, the name of Fleet will ever remain associated with *his* bantling, "Mother Goose."

And here it may not be deemed presumptuous of the publishers of this present volume to make a little comparison—and that as little odious as possible—between the mechanical and artistic chasm that yawns between the first production of " Mother Goose " and this, the last, which, with the reader's favor, stands as the apotheosis of " Mother Goose" in the book-making world!

CONTENTS.

ßistorical.

The traditional Nursery Rhymes of England commence with a legendary satire on King Cole, who reigned in Britain in the third century after Christ. According to Robert of Gloucester, he was the father of St. Helena. King Cole was a brave and popular man in his day.

OLD King Cole
Was a merry old soul,
And a merry old soul
      was he;

He called for his pipe,
And he called for his bowl,
And he called for his
      fiddlers three.

Every fiddler he had a fine fiddle,
And a very fine fiddle had he;
Twee tweedle dee, tweedle dee, went the fiddlers.
  Oh, there's none so rare
  As can compare
  With King Cole and his fiddlers three.

WHEN Arthur first in Court began
  To wear long hanging sleeves,
He entertained three servingmen
  And all of them were thieves.

The first he was an Irishman,
  The second was a Scot,
The third he was a Welshman,
  And all were knaves, I wot.

The Irishman loved usquebaugh,
  The Scot loved ale called bluecap,
The Welshman he loved toasted cheese,
  And made his mouth like a mouse-trap.

Usquebaugh burnt the Irishman;
  The Scot was drowned in ale;
The Welshman had like to be choked by a mouse,
  But he pulled it out by the tail.

Written on occasion of the marriage of Mary, the daughter of James,
Duke of York, afterwards James II., with the young Prince of Orange.

WHAT is the rhyme for *poringer* ?
The King he had a daughter fair,
And gave the Prince of Orange her.

LITTLE General Monk
  Sat upon a trunk,
Eating a crust of bread;
  There fell a hot coal
  And burnt in his clothes a hole,
Now General Monk is dead.
  Keep always from the fire:
  If it catch your attire,
You too, like Monk, will be dead

Robin Hood, Robin Hood,
Is in the mickle wood!
Little John, Little John,
He to the town is gone.
Robin Hood, Robin Hood,
Is telling his beads,
All in the greenwood,
Among the green weeds.
Little John, Little John,
If he comes no more,
Robin Hood, Robin Hood,
We shall fret fullsore!

The following perhaps refers to Joanna of Castile, who visited the Court of Henry VII., in the year 1506.

I HAD a little nut-tree,
nothing would it bear
But a silver nutmeg and
a golden pear;

The King of Spain's
daughter came to visit
me,
And all was because of
my little nut-tree.

I skipped over water, I
danced over sea,
And all the birds in the
air couldn't catch me.

Wʜᴇɴ good King Arthur ruled this land,
He was a goodly King;
He stole three pecks of barley-meal,
To make a bag-pudding.

A bag pudding the King
did make,
And stuffed it well
with plums,
And in it put great .umps
of fat,
As big as my two
thumbs.

The King and
Queen did
eat thereof,
And noble-
men beside;
And what they
could not eat
that night,
The Queen
next morn-
ing fried.

THE King of France, and four thousand men
They drew their swords—and put them up again.

In a tract called "Pigges Corantoe, or Newes from the North," 4to. Lond. 1642, p. 3, this is called "Old Tarlton's Song." It is perhaps a parody on the popular epigram of "Jack and Jill." I do not know the period of the battle to which it appears to allude, but Tarlton died in the year 1588.

THE King of France went up the hill,
   With twenty thousand men;
The King of France came down the hill,
   And ne'er went up again.

The King of France, with twenty thousand men,
Went up the hill, and then came down again.
The King of Spain, with twenty thousand more,
Climbed the same hill the French had climbed before.

Another version. The nurse sings the first line, and repeats it, time after time, until the expectant little one asks, What next? Then comes the climax.

The King of Francè, the King of France, with forty
    thousand men,
Oh, they all went up the hill, and so—came back again.

At the siege of Belleisle   All the while, all the while,
I was there all the while,   At the siege of Belleisle.

The rose is red, the grass is green,
Serve Queen Bess, our noble Queen;
    Kitty the spinner
    Will sit down to dinner,
And eat the leg of a frog;
    All good people
    Look over the steeple,
And see the cat play with the dog.

Good Queen Bess was a glorious dame,
When bonny King Jemmy from Scotland came;
    We'll pepper their bodies,
    Their peaceable noddies,
And give them a crack of the crown!

The twenty-ninth of May   Ring a ting ting,
Is oak-apple day.   God save the King.

The word *tory* originated in the reign of Elizabeth, and represented a class of "bog-trotters," who were a compound of the knave and the highwayman.

Ho! Master Teague, what is your story?
I went to the wood to kill a *tory ;*
I went to the wood and killed another;
Was it the same, or was it his brother?

I hunted him in, and I hunted him out,
Three times through the bog, about and about;
When out of a bush I saw his head,
So I fired my gun and shot him dead,

DOCTOR SACHEVEREL
Did very well,

But Jacky Dawbin
Gave him a warning.

The following nursery song alludes to William III. of England and George, Prince of Denmark.

WILLIAM and Mary, George and Anne,
Four such children had never a man:
They put their father to flight and shame,
And called their brother a shocking bad name.

A song on King William III.

As I walked by myself,
And talked to myself,
  Myself said unto me,
Look to thyself,
Take care of thyself,
  For nobody cares
      for thee.

I answered myself,
And said to myself,
  In the self-same repartee,
Look to thyself,
Or not look to thyself,
  The self-same thing
      will be.

From a MS. in the old Royal Library, in the British Museum. It is written in a hand of the time of Henry VIII., in an older manuscript.

We make no spare
Of John Hunkes' mare;
  And now I think she will die;
He thought it good
To put her in the wood,
  To seek where she might lie dry;
If the mare should chance to fail,
Then the crowns would for her sale.

Taken from MS. Douce, 357, fol. 124. See Echard's "History of England." Book III. chap. 1.

SEE saw, sack-a-day;
Monmouth is a pretie boy,
  Richmond is another,
Grafton is my only joy,
And why should I these three destroy,
  To please a pious brother ?

The following is partly quoted in an old song in a MS. at Oxford, Ashmole, No. 36, fol. 113.

As I was going by Charing Cross,
I saw a black man upon a black horse;
They told me it was King Charles the First;
Oh, dear! my heart was ready to burst!

Please to remember   I know no reason
The Fifth of November,   Why gunpowder treason
  Gunpowder treason and plot; Should ever be forgot.

HECTOR PROTECTOR was dressed all in green;
Hector Protector was sent to the Queen.
The Queen did not like him, nor more did the King;
So Hector Protector was sent back again.

From MS. Sloane, 1489, fol. 19, written in the time of Charles I. It appears from MS. Harl. 390, fol. 85, that these verses were written in 1626, against the Duke of Buckingham.

THERE was a monkey climbed up a tree,
When he fell down, then down fell he.

There was a crow sat on a stone,
When he was gone, then there was none.

There was an old wife did eat an apple,
When she had eat two, she had eat a couple.

There was a horse going to the mill,
When he went on, he stood not still.

There was a butcher cut his thumb,
When it did bleed, then blood did come.

There was a lackey ran a race,
When he ran fast, he ran apace.

There was a cobbler clouthing
    shoon,
When they were mended, they
    were done.

There was a chandler making
    candle,
When he them strip, he did
    them handle.

There was a navy went into
    Spain,
When it returned, it came
    again.

There was an old Crow set
    upon a Clod,
There is an end of my song—
    that's odd.

JIM and George were two great
    lords,
    They fought all in a churn;
And when that Jim got George
    by the nose,
    Then George began to gern.

EIGHTY-EIGHT wor Kirby feight,
    When niver a man was slain;
They yat ther meat, an drank ther drink,
    And sae com merrily heaam agayn.

Poor old Robinson Crusoe!
Poor old Robinson Crusoe!
They made him a coat
Of an old nanny goat
    I wonder how they could do so!
With a ring a ting tang,
And a ring a ting tang,
    Poor old Robinson Crusoe!

High diddle ding,
Did you hear the bells ring ?
The Parliament soldiers are gone to the King;
Some they did laugh, some they did cry,
To see the Parliament soldiers pass by.

High ding a ding, and ho ding a ding,
The Parliament soldiers are gone to the King;
Some with new beavers, some with new bands,
The Parliament soldiers are all to be hanged.

Over the water and over the lee,
And over the water to Charley,
Charley loves good ale and wine,
And Charley loves good brandy,
And Charley loves a pretty girl,
As sweet as sugar-candy.

Over the water, and over the sea,
And over the water to Charley,
I'll have none of your nasty beef,
Nor I'll have none of your barley;
But I'll have some of your very best flour,
To make a white cake for my Charley.

SECOND CLASS.

Literal.

One, two, three,
I love coffee,
And Billy loves tea.
How good you be,
One, two, three,
I love coffee,
And Billy loves tea.

F for fig,
J for jig,
    And N for
        knuckle-bones,
I for John
    the waterman,
And S for sack
        of stones.

1, 2, 3, 4, 5!
I caught a hare alive;
6, 7, 8, 9, 10!
I let her go again.

One, two,
Buckle my shoe;

Three, four,
Shut the door;

Five, six,
Pick up sticks;

Seven,
eight,
Lay them
straight;

Nine, ten,
A good fat hen;

Eleven,
twelve,
Who will
delve?

Thirteen,
fourteen,
Maids
a-courting;
Fifteen,
sixteen,
Maids
a-kissing;
Seventeen,
eighteen,
Maids
a-waiting;

Nineteen,
twenty,
My stomach's
empty.

AND **D,**

Pray, playmates agree.
E, F, and G,
Well, so it shall be.
J, K, and L,
In peace we will dwell.
M, N, and O,
To play let us go.

P, Q, R, and S,
Love may we possess.
W, X, and Y,
Will not quarrel or die.
Z, and amperse—and,
Go to school at command.

GREAT A, little a,
Bouncing B!
The cat's in the cupboard,
And she can't see.

———

AT reck'ning let's play,
And, prithee, let's lay
A wager, and let it be this:
Who first to the sum
Of twenty doth come,
Shall have for his winning a kiss.

———

TWENTY, nineteen, eighteen,
Seventeen, sixteen, fifteen,
Fourteen, thirteen, twelve,
Eleven, ten, nine,
Eight, seven, six,
Five, four, three,
Two, one;
The tenor o' the tune plays merrilie.

PAT-A-CAKE, pat-a-cake, baker's man!
So I will, master, as fast as I can:
Pat it, and prick it, and mark it with T,
Put in the oven for Tommy and me.

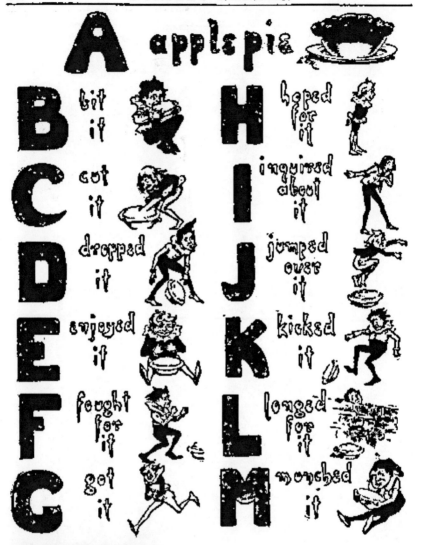

A apple pie

B bit it

C cut it

D dropped it

E enjoyed it

F fought for it

G got it

H hoped for it

I inquired about it

J jumped over it

K kicked it

L longed for it

M mouched it

A. B. C. tumble down D,
The cat's in the cupboard and
can't see me.

HICKERY, dickery, 6 and 7,
Alabone, Crackabone 10 and 11,
Spin span muskidan;
Twiddle 'um twaddle 'um, 21.

A was an angler,
  Went out in a fog;
Who fish'd all the day,
  And caught only a frog.

B was cook Betty,
  A-baking a pie
With ten or twelve apples
  All piled up on high.

C was a custard
  In a glass dish,
With as much cinnamon
  As you could wish.

D was fat Dick,
  Who did nothing but eat;
He would leave book and
          play
    For a nice bit of meat.

E was an egg,
  In a basket with more,
Which Peggy will sell
  For a shilling a score.

F was a fox,
  So cunning and sly:
Who looks at the hen-
          roost—
    I need not say why.

G was a greyhound,
  As fleet as the wind;
In the race or the course
  Left all others behind.

H was a heron,
  Who lived near a pond;
Of gobbling the fishes
  He was wondrously fond.

I was the ice
  On which Billy would
      skate;
So up went his heels,
  And down went his pate.

J was Joe Jenkins,
  Who played on the fiddle;
He began twenty tunes,
  But left off in the middle.

K was a kitten,
  Who jumped at a cork,
And learned to eat mice
  Without plate, knife, or
      fork.

L was a lark,
  Who sings us a song,
And wakes us betimes
  Lest we sleep too long.

M was Miss Molly,
  Who turned in her toes,
And hung down her head
  Till her knees touched
      her nose.

N was a nosegay,
  Sprinkled with dew,
Pulled in the morning
  And presented to you.

O was an owl,
  Who looked wondrously
      wise;
But he's watching a mouse
  With his large round eyes.

P was a parrot,
  With feathers like gold,
Who talks just as much,
  And no more than he's
      told.

Q is the Queen
  Who governs the land,
And sits on a throne
  Very lofty and grand.

R is a raven
  Perched on an oak,
Who with a gruff voice
  Cries Croak, croak, croak!

S was a stork
  With a very long bill,
Who swallows down fishes
  And frogs to his fill.

T is a trumpeter
  Blowing his horn,
Who tells us the news
  As we rise in the
      morn.

U is a unicorn,
　Who, as it is said,
Wears an ivory bodkin
　On his forehead.

V is a vulture
　Who eats a great deal,
Devouring a dog
　Or a cat as a meal.

W was a watchman
　Who guarded the
　　street,
Lest robbers or
　　thieves
　The good people
　　should meet.

X was King Xerxes,
　Who, if you don't
　　know,
Reigned over Persia
　A great while ago.

Y is the year
　That is passing away,
And still growing shorter
　Every day.

Z is a zebra,
　Whom you've heard of
　　before;
So here ends my rhyme
　Till I find you some more.

　　ONE's none;
　　Two's some;
　　Three's a many;
　　Four's a penny;
　　Five is a little hundred.

WHO is that I heard call ?　Little Sam in the hall.
What does he do there ?　He asked for some fruit.
For some fruit did he ask ?　Can he yet read his book ?
He can't read it yet; then he shan't have a bit.
But pray give him a bite when he says his task right;
And till that is well done, take you care he has none.

Tom Thumb's Alphabet.

A was an Archer, and shot at a frog,
B was a Butcher, and had a great dog,
C was a Captain, all covered with lace,
D was a Drunkard, and had a red face.
E was an Esquire, with pride on his brow,
F was a Farmer, and followed the plough,
G was a Gamester, who had but ill luck,
H was a Hunter, and hunted a buck.
I was an Innkeeper, who loved to bouse,
J was a Joiner, and built up a house.
K was King William, once governed this land,
L was a Lady, who had a white hand.
M was a Miser, and hoarded up gold,
N was a Nobleman, gallant and bold.
O was an Oyster Wench, and went about town,
P was a Parson, and wore a black gown.
Q was a Queen, who was fond of good flip,
R was a Robber, and wanted a whip,
S was a Sailor, and spent all he got,
T was a Tinker, and mended a pot.
U was an Usurer, a miserable elf,
V was a Vintner, who drank all himself.
W was a Watchman, and guarded the door,
X was expensive, and so became poor.
Y was a Youth, that did not love school,
Z was a Zany, a poor harmless fool.

APPLE-PIE, pudding, and pancake,
All begin with A.

Miss One, Two, and Three could never agree,
While they gossiped round a tea-caddy.

Come hither, little puppy dog;
 I'll give you a new collar,
If you will learn to read your
  book
And be a clever scholar.
No, no! replied the puppy dog,
 I've other fish to fry,
For I must learn to guard
  your house,
 And bark when thieves
 come nigh.
With a tingle, tangle, tit-
  mouse!
 Robin knows great A,
And B, and C, and D, and E,
 F, G, H, I. J, K.

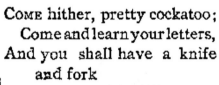

Come hither, pretty cockatoo;
 Come and learn your letters,
And you shall have a knife
  and fork
 To eat with, like your
 betters.
No, no! the cockatoo replied,
 My beak will do as well;
I'd rather eat my victuals thus
 Than go and learn to spell.
With a tingle, tangle, tit-
  mouse!
 Robin knows great A,
And B, and C, and D, and E,
 F, G, H, I, J, K.

Come hither, little pussy cat;
If you'll your grammar
    study
I'll give you silver clogs to
    wear,
Whene'er the gutter's
    muddy
No! whilst I grammar learn,
    says Puss,
Your house will in a trice
Be overrun from top to bottom
With flocks of rats and mice.
With a tingle, tangle, tit-
    mouse!
Robin knows great A,
And B, and C, and D, and E,
F, G, H, I, J, K.

Come hither, then, good little
    boy,
And learn your alphabet,
And you a pair of boots and
    spurs,
Like your papa's, shall get,
Oh, yes! I'll learn my alpha-
    bet;
And when I well can read,
Perhaps papa will give, me too,
A pretty long-tail'd steed.
With a tingle, tangle, tit-
    mouse!
Robin knows great A,
And B, and C, and D, and E,
F, G, H, I, J, K.

A for the ape, that we saw at the fair;
B for a blockhead, who ne'er shall go there;
C for a cauliflower, white as a curd;
D for a duck, a very good bird;
E for an egg, good in pudding or pies;
F for a farmer, rich, honest, and wise;
G for a gentleman, void of all care;
H for the hound, that ran down the hare;
I for an Indian, soothy and dark;
K for the keeper, that looked to the park;
L for a lark, that soared in the air;
M for a mole, ne'er could get there;
N for Sir Nobody, ever in fault;
O for an otter, that ne'er could be caught;
P for a pudding, stuck full of plums;
Q was for quartering it, see here he comes;
R for a rook, that croaked in the trees;
S for a sailor, that ploughed the deep seas;
T for a top, that doth prettily spin;
V for a virgin, of delicate mien;
W for wealth, in gold, silver, and pence;
X for old Xenophone, noted for sense;
Y for a yew, which for ever is green;
Z for the zebra, that belongs to the Queen.

THIRD CLASS.

Tales.

SOLOMON GRUNDY,
Born on a Monday,
Christened on Tuesday,
Married on Wednesday,
Took ill on Thursday,
Worse on Friday,
Died on Saturday,
Buried on Sunday;
This is the end
Of Solomon Grundy.

HAVE you ever heard of Billy Pringle's pig?
It was very little and not very big;
When it was alive it lived in clover;
But now it's dead, and that's all over.
Billy Pringle he lay down and died,
Betsy Pringle she sat down and cried;
So there's an end of all the three,
Billy Pringle he, Betsy Pringle she, and poor little piggy
wigee.

My dear, do you know,
How, a long time ago,
   Two poor little children,
Whose names I don't know,
Were stolen away on a fine summer's day,
And left in a wood, as I've heard people say.

And when it was night,
So sad was their plight,
   The sun it went down,
And the moon gave no light !
They sobbed and they sighed, and they bitterly cried,
And the poor little things, they lay down and died.

And when they were dead,
The Robins so red
   Brought strawberry-leaves
And over them spread;

And all the day long
They sung them this song :
"Poor babes in the wood ! Poor babes in the wood!
And don't you remember the babes in the wood?"

THERE was a fat man of Bombay,
Who was smoking one sunshiny day,
  When a bird, called a snipe,
  Flew away with his pipe,
Which vexed the fat man of Bombay.

LITTLE Tom Tittlemouse lived in a bell-house;
The bell-house broke, and Tom Tittlemouse woke.

PUNCH and Judy   Punch gave Judy
  Fought for a pie;   A sad blow on the eye.

ROBIN the Bobbin, the big-headed Ben,
He ate more meat than fourscore men;
He ate a cow, he ate a calf,
He ate a butcher and a half;
He ate a church, he ate a steeple,
He ate the priest and all the people !
      A cow and a calf,
      An ox and a half,
      A church and a steeple,
      And all the good people,
And yet he complained that his stomach wasn't full.

THERE was a jolly miller   You have been biting me,
  Lived on the River Dee;   And you must die."
He looked upon his pillow,   So he cracked his bones
  And there he saw a flea.   Upon the stones,
"Oh, Mr. Flea,   And there he let him lie.

Simple Simon met a pieman,
  Going to the fair;
Says Simple Simon to the pieman,
  "Let me taste your ware."

Says the pieman to Simple Simon,
  "Show me first your penny."

Says Simple Simon to the pieman,
"Indeed I have not any."

Simple Simon went a-fishing
 For to catch a whale;
All the water he had got
 Was in his mother's pail.

LITTLE Jack Jelf
Was put on the shelf
Because he would not spell
 "pie;"
When his aunt, Mrs.
 Grace,
Saw his sorrowful face,
She could not help saying,
 "Oh, fie!"

And since Master Jelf
Was put on the shelf
Because he would not spell
 "pie,"
Let him stand there so
 grim,
And no more about him,
For I wish him a very good
 bye!

LITTLE Tommy Tittlemouse
Lived in a little house:

He caught fishes
In other men's ditches.

THERE was a crooked man, and he went a crooked mile,
He found a crooked sixpence against a crooked stile:
He bought a crooked cat, which caught a crooked
     mouse,
And they all lived together in a little crooked house.

THERE was a man, and he had nought,
　And robbers came to rob him;
He crept up to the chimney-pot,
　And then they thought they had him.

But he got down on t'other side,
　And then they could not find him.
He ran fourteen miles in fifteen days,
　And never looked behind him.

THERE was a little man,
And he had a little gun,
And he went to the brook,
And he shot a little rook;

And he took it home
To his old wife Joan,
And told her to make up a
    fire,

While he went back   The drake was fled for fear;
To fetch the little drake;   And, like an old novice, he
But when he got there,   turned back again.

Two little dogs   Said one little dog
Sat by the fire,   To the other little dog,
Over a fender of coal-dust;   If you don't talk, why, I must.

BRYAN O'Lin and his wife and wife's mother,
They all went over a bridge together:
The bridge was broken, and they all fell in,
"The deuce go with all!" quoth Bryan O'Lin.

LITTLE Tom Twig bought a fine bow and arrow,
And what did he shoot? why, a poor little sparrow.
Oh, fie, little Tom, with your fine bow and arrow,
How cruel to shoot at a poor little sparrow!

OLD Mother Goose, when
  She wanted to wander,
Would ride through the air
  On a very fine gander.

Mother Goose had a house,
  'Twas built in a wood,
Where an owl at the door
  For sentinel stood.

She sent him to market,
  A live goose he bought:
"Here! mother," says he,
  "It will not go for
    nought."

Jack's goose and her gander
  Grew very fond;
They'd both eat together,
  Or swim in one pond.

Jack found one morning,
  As I have been told,
His goose had laid him
  An egg of pure gold.

Jack rode to his mother,
  The news for to tell.
She called him a good boy,
  And said it was well.

Jack sold his gold egg
  To a rogue of a Jew,
Who cheated him out of
  The half of his due.

Then Jack went a-courting
  A lady so gay,
As fair as the lily,
  And sweet as the May.

The Jew and the Squire
  Came behind his back,
And began to belabor
  The sides of poor Jack.

The old Mother Goose,
  That instant came in,
And turned her son Jack
  Into famed Harlequin.

She then with her wand
  Touched the lady so fine,
And turned her at once
  Into sweet Columbine.

The gold egg into the sea
  Was thrown then,—
When Jack jumped in,
  And got the egg back
    again.

The Jew got the goose,
  Which he vowed he
    would kill,
Resolving at once
  His pockets to fill.

Jack's mother came in,
  And caught the goose
    soon,
And mounting its back,
Flew up to the moon.

WHEN I was a little girl, about seven years old,
I hadn't got a petticoat to cover me from the cold;
So I went into Darlington, that pretty little town,
And there I bought a petticoat, a cloak, and a gown,
I went into the woods and built me a kirk,
And all the birds of the air, they helped me to work.
The hawk with his long claws pulled down the stone,
The dove, with her rough bill, brought me them home:
The parrot was the clergyman, the peacock was the clerk,
The bullfinch played the organ, and we made merry work.

ROBIN and Richard were two pretty men;
They lay in bed till the clock struck ten;
Then up starts Robin and looks at the sky;
Oh! brother Richard, the sun's very high:
The bull's in the barn threshing the corn;
The cock's on the dunghill blowing his horn,
The cat's at the fire frying of fish,
The dog's in the pantry breaking his dish.

THREE wise men of Gotham went to sea in a bowl,
And if the bowl had been stronger, my song would have
been longer.

WHEN little
Fred went
to bed
He always
said his
prayers.
He kissed
mamma and
then papa,
And straight-
way went
upstairs.

LITTLE Willie Winkle runs through the town,
Upstairs and downstairs, in his nightgown,
Rapping at the window, crying through the lock,
"Are the children in their beds? for now it's eight
o'clock."

Pemmy was a pretty girl,
  But Fanny was a better;
Pemmy looked like any churl,
  When little Fanny let her.

Pemmy had a pretty nose,
  But Fanny had a better;
Pemmy oft would come to blows,
  But Fanny would not let her.

Pemmy had a pretty doll,
  But Fanny had a better;
Pemmy chattered like a poll,
  When little Fanny let her.

Pemmy had a pretty song,
  But Fanny had a better,
Pemmy would sing all day long,
  But Fanny would not let her.

Pemmy loved a pretty lad,
  And Fanny loved a better;
And Pemmy wanted for to wed,
  But Fanny would not let her.

———

Our saucy boy Dick
Had a nice little stick
  Cut from a hawthorn
    tree,
And with this pretty stick
He thought he could beat
  A boy much bigger than
    he.

But the boy turned round,
And hit him a rebound.
  Which did so frighten
    poor Dick,
That, without more delay,
He ran quite away,
  And over a hedge he
    jumped quick.

THE lion and the unicorn
Were fighting for the
crown;
The lion beat the uni-
corn
All round about the
town.
Some gave them white
bread,
And some gave them
brown;
Some gave them plum
cake,
And sent them out of
town.

Moss was a little man, and a little mare did buy,
For kicking and for sprawling none her could come nigh;
She could trot, she could amble, and could canter here
and there;
But one night she strayed away—so Moss lost his mare.

Moss got up next morning to catch her fast asleep,
And round about the frosty fields so nimbly he did creep.
Dead in a ditch he found her, and glad to find her there,
So I'll tell you, by-and-bye, how Moss caught his mare.

"Rise! stupid, rise!" he thus to her did say;
"Arise, you beast, you drowsy beast, get up without
delay,
For I must ride you to the town, so don't lie sleeping
there."
He put the halter round her neck—so Moss caught his
mare.

LITTLE King Boggen he built a fine hall,
Pie-crust and pastry-crust, that was the wall;
The windows were made of black-puddings and white,
And slated with pancakes;—you ne'er saw the like.

Taffy was a Welshman, Taffy was a thief;
Taffy came to my house and stole a piece of beef;
I went to Taffy's house, Taffy was not at home;
Taffy came to my house and stole a marrow-bone.

I went to Taffy's house, Taffy was not in;
Taffy came to my house and stole a silver pin;
I went to Taffy's house, Taffy was in bed,
I took up a poker and flung it at his head.

Doctor Foster went to Glo'ster
In a shower of rain;
He stepped in a puddle, up to the middle,
And never went there again.

Tommy kept a chandler's shop,
Richard went to buy a mop,
Tommy gave him such a knock,
That sent him out of his chandler's shop.

Tom, Tom, the piper's son,
   Stole a pig, and away he run;
The pig was eat, and Tom was beat,
   And Tom ran roaring down the street.

Little Blue Betty lived in a lane,
She sold good ale to gentlemen:

Gentlemen came every day,
And little Betty Blue hopped away.
She hopped upstairs to make her bed,
And she tumbled down and broke her head.

THE man in the moon
Came tumbling down,
And asked his way to Norwich:
He went by the south,
And burnt his mouth
With supping cold pease-porridge.

My Lady Wind, my Lady Wind,
Went round about the house to find
    A chink to get her foot in:
She tried the key-hole in the door,
She tried the crevice in the floor,
    And drove the chimney soot in.

And then one night when it was dark,
She blew up such a tiny spark
    That all the house was pothered:
From it she raised up such a flame
As flamed away to Belting Lane,
    And White Cross folks were smothered.

And thus when once, my little dears,
A whisper reaches itching ears,
    The same will come, you'll find:
Take my advice, restrain the tongue,
Remember what old Nurse has sung
    Of busy Lady Wind!

OLD Abram Brown is dead and gone,
    You'll never see him more;
He used to wear a long brown coat,
    That buttoned down before.

The Queen of Hearts, she made some tarts,
   All on a summer's day;
The Knave of Hearts, he stole the tarts,
   And took them clean away.

The King of Hearts called for the tarts,
   And beat the Knave full sore;

The Knave of Hearts brought back the tarts,
And vowed he'd steal no more.

THERE was an old man of Cantyre,
Who always stood back to the fire,
And was quite at a loss
To know why folks looked cross;
That selfish old man of Cantyre.

I HAD a little hobby-
horse,
And it was dapple
grey;
Its head was made of
pea-straw,
Its tail was made of
hay.

I sold it to an old
woman
For a copper groat;
And I'll not sing my
song again
Without a new coat.

The rhyme of Jack Horner has been stated to be a satire on the Puri-
tanical aversion to Christmas pies and such-like abominations.   It forms
part of a metrical chap-book history, founded on the same story as the
Friar and the Boy, entitled "The Pleasant History of Jack Horner, containing his witty tricks and pleasant pranks which he played from his
youth to his riper years: right pleasant and delightful for winter and
summer's recreation," embellished with frightful woodcuts, which have
not much connection with the tale.   The pleasant history commences as
follows:

Jack Horner was a pretty lad,
 Near London he did dwell,
His father's heart he made full glad,
 His mother lov'd him well.
While little Jack was sweet and young,
 If he by chance should cry,
His mother pretty sonnets sung.
 With a lul-la-ba-by.

With such a dainty curious tone,
 As Jack sat on her knee,
So that ere he could go alone
 He sang as well as she.
A pretty boy of curious wit,
 All people spoke his praise,
And in the corner would he sit
 In Christmas holidays.

When friends they did together meet
To pass away the time,
Why, little Jack, he sure would eat
His Christmas pie in rhyme.

And said, Jack Horner, in the corner,
Eats good Christmas pie,
And with his thumbs pulls out the plums,
And said, Good boy am I!

Here we have an important discovery! Who before ever suspected that the nursery rhyme was written by Jack Horner himself?

LITTLE Jack Horner sat in the corner,
　　Eating a Christmas pie;

He put in his thumb, and took out a plum,
　　And said, "What a good boy am I!"

THERE was an old woman who rode on a broom,
   With a high gee ho, gee humble;
And she took her old cat behind for a groom,
   With a bimble, bamble, bumble.

They travelled along till they came to the sky,
   With a high gee ho, gee humble;
But the journey so long made them very hungry,
   With a bimble, bamble, bumble.

Says Tom, "I can find nothing here to eat,
   With a high gee ho, gee humble;
So let us go back again, I entreat,
   With a bimble, bamble, bumble."

The old woman would not go back so soon,
   With a high gee ho, gee humble;
For she wanted to visit the Man in the Moon,
   With a bimble, bamble, bumble.

Says Tom, "I'll go back by myself to our house,
   With a high gee ho, gee humble;
For there I can catch a good rat or a mouse,
   With a bimble, bamble, bumble."

"But," says the old woman, "how will you go?
   With a high gee ho, gee humble;
You shan't have my nag, I protest and vow,
   With a bimble, bamble, bumble."

" No, no," says Tom, "I've a plan of my own,
   With a high gee ho, gee humble;"
So he slid down the rainbow, and left her alone,
   With a bimble, bamble, bumble.

So now, if you happen to visit the sky,
   With a high gee ho, gee humble,
And want to come back, you Tom's method may try,
   With a bimble, bamble, bumble.

A DOG and a cock a journey once took,
  They travelled along till 't was late;
The dog he made free in the hollow of a tree;
  And the cock on the boughs of it sate.

  The cock, nothing knowing,
  In the morn fell a-crowing,
Upon which comes a fox to the tree,
  Says he, "I declare
  Your voice is above
All the creatures I ever did see.

  Oh, would you come down,
  I the fav'rite might own!"
Said the cock, "There's a porter below;
  If you will go in,
  I promise I'll come down."
So he went—and was worried for it too.

THERE was a King, and he had three daughter,
And they all lived in a basin of water;
    The basin bended,
    My story's ended.
If the basin had been stronger
My story would have been longer.

FOURTH CLASS

Proverbs.

St. Swithin's Day, if thou dost rain,
For forty days it will remain:
St. Swithin's Day, if thou be fair,
For forty days 't will rain na mair.

———

Bounce Buckram, velvet's dear:
Christmas comes but once a year.

———

Shoe the horse and shoe the mare;
But let the little colt go bare.

———

[Hours of sleep.]

Nature requires five;
Custom gives seven;

Laziness takes nine,
And Wickedness eleven.

To make your candles last for aye,
  You wives and maids give ear-o!
To put 'em out's the only way,
  Says honest John Boldero.

A SWARM of bees in May
Is worth a load of hay;

A swarm of bees in June   A swarm of bees in July
Is worth a silver spoon;   Is not worth a fly.

IF wishes were horses,
  Beggars would ride;
If turnips were watches,
  I would wear one by my side.

A MAN of words and not of deeds,
Is like a garden full of weeds;
And when the weeds begin to grow,
It's like a garden full of snow;
And when the snow begins to fall,
It's like a bird upon the wall;
And when the bird away does fly,
It's like an eagle in the sky;
And when the sky begins to roar,
It's like a lion at the door;
And when the door begins to crack,
It's like a stick across your back;
And when your back begins to smart,
It's like a penknife in your heart;
And when your heart begins to bleed,
You're dead, and dead, and dead indeed.

A MAN of words and not of deeds,
Is like a garden full of weeds;
For when the weeds begin to grow,
Then doth the garden overflow.

FOR every every evil under the sun
There is a remedy, or there is none.
If there be one, try and find it;
If there be none, never mind it.

NEEDLES and pins,
   needles and pins,
When a man marries
   his trouble begins.

A SUNSHINY shower
Won't last half an
            hour.

A PULLET in the pen
Is worth a hundred in the fen.

IF you sneeze on Monday, you sneeze for danger;
Sneeze on a Tuesday, kiss a stranger;
Sneeze on a Wednesday, sneeze for a letter;
Sneeze on a Thursday, something better;
Sneeze on a Friday, sneeze for sorrow;
Sneeze on a Saturday, see your sweetheart to-morrow.

THEY that wash on Monday
   Have all the week to dry;
They that wash on Tuesday
   Are not so much awry;
They that wash on Wednesday
   Are not so much to blame;
They that wash on Thursday,
   Wash for shame;
They that wash on Friday,
   Wash in need;
And they that wash on Saturday,
   Oh! they're sluts indeed.

As the days grow longer
The storms grow stronger.

WHEN the wind is in the east,
'T is neither good for man nor beast;

When the wind is in the north,
The skilful fisher goes not forth;

When the wind is in
the south,
It blows the bait in
the fishes' mouth;

When the wind is in
the west,
Then 't is at the very
best.

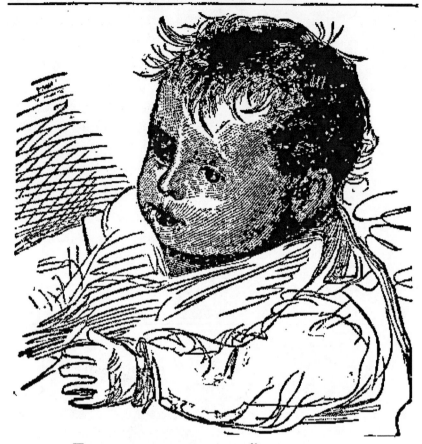

THREE straws on a staff,
Would make a baby cry and laugh.

SEE a pin and pick it up,
All the day you'll have good luck;
See a pin and let it lay,
Bad luck you'll have all the day.

Go to bed first, a golden purse;
Go to bed second, a golden pheasant;
Go to bed third, a golden bird!

As the days lengthen
So the storms strengthen.

In Suffolk, children are often reminded of the decorum due to the Sabbath by the following lines.

YEOW mussent sing a' Sunday,
Becaze it is a sin,
But yeow may sing a' Monday
Till Sunday cums agin.

HE that goes to see his wheat in May,
Comes weeping away.

LAZY Lawrence, let me go,
Don't hold me summer and winter too.

This distich is said by a boy who feels very lazy, yet wishes to exert himself. Lazy Lawrence is a proverbial expression for an idle person, and there is an old chap-book, entitled "the History of Lawrence Lazy, containing his birth and slotful breeding; how he served the school-master, his wife, the squire's cook, and the farmer, which, by the laws of Lubberland, was accounted high treason." A west country proverb, relating to a disciple of this hero, runs thus:

Sluggardy guise,
Loth to go to bed,
And loth to rise.

H‍ᴇ that would thrive   He that hath thriven
Must rise at five;   May lie till seven;
    And he that by the plough would thrive,
    Himself must either hold or drive.

Iɴ July,   In August,
Some reap rye;   If one will not the other
                   must.

Proverbial many years ago, when the guinea in gold was of a higher
value than its nominal representative in silver.

    A ɢᴜɪɴᴇᴀ it would sink,
      And a pound it would float;
    Yet I'd rather have a guinea,
      Than your one pound note.

Tʜᴇ art of good driving is a paradox quite,
    Though custom has proved it so long:
If you go to the left, you're sure to go right,
    If you go to the right, you go wrong.

    Tʜᴇ mackerel's cry
    Is never long dry.

The proverb of *tit for tat* may perhaps be said to be going out of fashion, but it is still a universal favorite with children. When any one is ill-natured, and the sufferer wishes to hint his intention of retaliating at the first convenient opportunity, he cries out—

TIT for tat,
If you kill my dog,
I'll kill your cat.

MARCH will search,
April will try,
May will tell ye if ye'll
live or die.

WHEN the sand doth feed the clay,
England woe and well-a-day!
But when the clay doth feed the sand,
Then it is well with Angle-land.

A CAT may look at a King,
And surely I may look at an ugly thing.
Said in derision by one child to another, who complains of being stared at.

FRIDAY night's dream
On the Saturday told,
Is sure to come true,
Be it never so old.

TRIM tram,
Like master like man.

From an old manuscript political treatise, dated 1652, entitled "A Cat may look at a King."

He that hath it and will not keep it,
He that wanteth it and will not seek it,
He that drinketh and is not dry,
Shall want money as well as I.

From Howell's English Proverbs, 1659, p. 21.

Sow in the sop,
'T will be heavy a-top.

That is, land in a soppy or wet state is in a favorable condition for re-
ceiving seed; a statement, however, somewhat questionable.

Gray's Inn for walks,
Lincoln's Inn for a wall,
The Inner-Temple for a garden,
And the Middle for a hall.

A proverb, no doubt, true in former times, but now only partially correct.

In time of prosperity friends will be plenty,
In time of adversity not one amongst twenty.

From Howell's English Proverbs, p. 20. The expression, *not one
amongst twenty*, is a generic one for not one out of a large number. It
occurs in Shakespeare's "Much Ado About Nothing," V., 2.

Beer a bumble,
'T will kill you
Afore 't will make ye tumble.

A proverbial phrase applied to very small beer, an home brewed
beverage formerly very common in the rural parts of England, implying
that no quantity of it will cause intoxication.

The fair maid who, the first of May,
Goes to the fields at break of day,
And washes in dew from the hawthorn-tree,
Will ever after handsome be.

FIFTH CLASS.

Scholastic.

A DILLER, a dollar,
  A ten o'clock scholar,
What makes you come so
    soon?
  You used to come at ten
    o'clock,
But now you come at noon.

———

SPEAK when you're spoken
    to,
  Come when one call,
Shut the door after you,
  And turn to the wall.

———

BIRCH and green holly,
    boys,
  Birch and green holly.
If you get beaten, boys,
  'T will be your own folly.

TELL tale, tit!
Your tongue shall be slit,
And all the dogs in the town
Shall have a little bit.

A Greek bill of fare.

LEGOMOTON,
Acapon,
Afatgheuse,
Pasti venison.

The joke of the following consists in saying it so quick that it cannot be told whether it is English or gibberish. It was a schoolboy's rhyme in the fifteenth century.

IN fir tar is,	In clay none is.
In oak none is.	Goat eat ivy,
In mud eel is,	Mare eat oats.

The dominical letters attached to the first days of the several months are remembered by the following lines:

At Dover Dwells George Brown Esquire,
Good Christopher Finch, And David Friar.

COME when you're called,
Do what you're bid,
Shut the door after you,
Never be chid.

THE rose is red,
The grass is green;
And in this book
My name is seen.

MULTIPLICATION is vexation,
  Division is as bad;
The Rule of Three doth puzzle me,
  And Practice drives me mad.

CROSS-PATCH,
Draw the latch,
Sit by the fire and spin;

Take a cup,
And drink it up,
Then call your neighbors
in.

Doctor Faustus was a good
man,
He whipped his scholars now
and then;
When he whipped them he made
them dance
Out of Scotland into France,
Out of France into Spain,
And then he whipped them back
again!

When I was a little boy I had
but little wit;
It is some time ago, and I've no
more yet;
Nor ever ever shall until that I
die,
For the longer I live the more
fool am I.

The following memorial lines are by no means modern. They occur,
with slight variations, in an old play called "The Returne from Parnas-
sus," 4to. Lond. 1606.

Thirty days hath September,
April, June, and November;
February has twenty-eight alone,
All the rest have thirty-one,
Excepting Leap-year, that's the time
When February's days are twenty-nine.

A laconic reply to a person who indulges much in supposition.

If "ifs" and "ands"
Were pots and pans,
There would be no need for tinkers!

MISTRESS MARY, quite contrary,
How does your garden grow?
With cockle-shells and silver bells
And mussels all a-row.

My story's ended,
My spoon is bended:
If you don't like it,

Go to the next door
And get it mended.

On arriving at the end of a book, boys have a practice of reciting the following absurd lines, which form the word *finis* backward and forwards by the initials of the words.

FATHER IOHNSON Nicholas Iohnson's Son—
Son Iohnson Nicholas Iohnson's Father.

To "get to Father Johnson," therefore, was to reach the end of the book.

WHEN V and I together meet,
They make the number Six complete.
When I with V doth meet once more,
Then 't is they Two can make but Four.
And when that V from I is gone,
Alas! poor I can make but One.

SIXTH CLASS.

Songs.

OH, where are you going,
  My pretty maiden fair,
With your red rosy cheeks,
  And your coal-black
                 hair?
I'm going a-milking,
  Kind sir, says she,
And it's dabbling in the dew
  Where you'll find me.

May I go with you,
  My pretty maiden fair,
              etc.
Oh, you may go with me,
  Kind sir, says she, etc.

If I should chance to kiss
              you,
  My pretty maiden fair,
              etc.
The wind may take it off
             again,
  Kind sir, says she, etc.

And what is your father,
  My pretty maiden fair?
              etc.
My father's a farmer,
  Kind sir, says she, etc.

And what is your mother,
  My pretty maiden fair?

With your red rosy cheeks,   My mother's a dairymaid,
  And your coal-black   Kind sir, says she,
              hair?   And it's dabbling in the dew
                                 Where you'll find me.

WHERE are you going, my pretty maid,
   With your rosy cheeks and golden hair?
"I'm going a-milking, sir," she said;
   The strawberry-leaves make maidens fair.

Shall I go with you, my pretty maid,
   With your rosy cheeks and golden hair?
" Yes, if you please, kind sir," she said;
   The strawberry-leaves make maidens fair.

What is your father, my pretty maid,
   With your rosy cheeks and golden hair?
" My father's a farmer, sir," she said;
   The strawberry-leaves make maidens fair.

What is your fortune, my pretty maid,
   With your rosy cheeks and golden hair?
" My face is my fortune, sir," she said;
   The strawberry-leaves make maidens fair.

Then I won't have you, my pretty maid,
   With your rosy cheeks and golden hair.
" Nobody asked you, sir," she said;
   The strawberry-leaves make maidens fair.

You shall have an apple,
   You shall have a plum,
You shall have a rattle-basket,
   When your dad comes home.

LEND me thy mare to ride a mile?
She is lamed, leaping over a stile.
Alack! and I must keep the fair!
I'll give thee money for thy mare.
Oh, oh! say you so?
Money will make the mare to go.

UP at Piccadilly oh! the coachman takes his stand,
And when he meets a pretty girl, he takes her by the hand;
Whip away for ever oh! drive away so clever oh!
All the way to Bristol oh! he drives her four-in-hand.

Polly, put the kettle on,
Polly, put the kettle on,
Polly, put the kettle on,
  And let's drink tea.

Sukey, take it off again,
Sukey, take it off again,
Sukey, take it off again,
  They're all gone away.

Jeanie come tie my,
  Jeanie come tie my,
Jeanie come tie my bonnie
                  cravat;
  I've tied it behind,
  I've tied it before,
And I've tied it so often, I'll
            tie it no more.

The original of the following is to be found in " Deuteromelia, or the second part of Mūsicks Melodie," 4to, Lond. 1609, where the music is also given.

THREE blind mice,
see how they run!
They all ran after
the farmer's wife,
Who cut off their
tails with the
carving-knife;
Did you ever see
such fools in your
life?
Three blind mice.

THE fox and his wife they had a great strife,
The never ate mustard in all their whole life;
They ate their meat without fork or knife,
And loved to be picking a bone, e-ho!

The fox jumped up on a moonlight night,
The stars they were shining, and all things bright;
Oh, ho! said the fox, it's a very fine night
For me to go through the town, e-ho!

The fox when he came to yonder stile,
He lifted his lugs and he listened awhile;
Oh, ho! said the fox, it's but a short mile
From this unto yonder wee town, e-ho!

The fox when he came to the farmer's gate,
Who should he see but the farmer's drake:
I love you well for your master's sake,
And long to be picking your bone, e-ho!

Then the old man got up in his red cap,
And swore he would catch the fox in a trap;
But the fox was too cunning, and gave him the slip,
And ran thro' the town, the town, e-oh!

When he got to the top of the hill,
He blew his trumpet both loud and shrill,
For joy that he was safe
    Through the town, e-oh!

When the fox came back to his den,
He had young ones both nine and ten,
" You're welcome home, daddy; you may go again,
If you bring us such nice meat
    From the town, e-oh!"

The grey goose she ran round the hay-stack,
Oh, ho! said the fox, you are very fat;
You'll grease my beard and ride on my back
    From this into yonder wee town, e-ho!

Old Gammer Hipple-hopple hopped out of bed,
She opened the casement, and popped out her head;
Oh! husband, oh! husband, the grey goose is dead,
    And the fox is gone through the town, oh!

ONE misty moisty morning
    When cloudy was the weather,
There I met an old man
    Clothed all in leather;
    Clothed all in leather,
    With cap under his chin,—
How do you do, and how do you do,
    And how do you do again?

From W. Wager's play, called "The longer thou livest, the more foole
        thou art," 4to, Lond.

THE white dove sat on the castle wall,
I bend my bow and shoot her I shall;
I put her in my glove both feathers and all;
I laid my bridle upon the shelf,
If you will any more, sing it yourself.

Little Tom Dogget,
　What does thou mean,
To kill thy poor Colly
　Now she's so lean?
Sing, oh poor Colly,
　Colly, my cow;
For Colly will give me
　No more milk now.

I had better have kept her
　Till fatter she had been,
For now, I confess,
　She's a little too lean.
Sing, oh poor Colly, etc.

First in comes the tanner
　With his sword by his
　　　　side,
And he bids me five shil-
　　　lings,
　For my poor cow's hide.
Sing, oh poor Colly, etc.

Then in comes the tallow-
　　　chandler,
Whose brains were but
　　　shallow,
And he bids me two-and-
　　　sixpence
　For my cow's tallow.
Sing, oh poor Colly, etc.

Then in comes the hunts-
　　　man
　So early in the morn,
He bids me a penny
　For my cow's horn.
Sing, oh poor Colly, etc.

Then in comes the tripe-
　　　woman,
　So fine and so neat,
She bids me three half-
　　　pence
　For my cow's feet.
Sing, oh poor Colly, etc.

Then in comes the butcher,
　That nimble-tongued
　　　　youth,
Who said she was carrion,
　But he spoke not the
　　　　truth.
Sing, oh poor Colly, etc.

The skin of my cowly
　Was softer than silk,
And three times a day
　My poor cow would
　　　　give milk.
Sing, oh poor Colly, etc.

She every year
　A fine calf did me bring,
Which fetched me a pound,
　For it came in the spring.
Sing, oh poor Colly, etc.

But now I have killed her
　I can't her recall;
I will sell my poor Colly,
　Hide, horns and all.
Sing, oh poor Colly, etc.

The butcher shall have her,
　Though he gives but a
　　　　pound,
And he knows in his heart
　That my Colly was
　　　　sound.
Sing, oh poor Colly, etc.

And when he has bought
　　　　her,
　Let him sell altogether
The flesh for to eat,
　And the hide for leather.
Sing, oh poor Colly, etc.

A different version from the above, commencing, "My Billy Aroma," is current in the nurseries of Cornwall. One verse runs as follows:

> In comes the horner,
> 　Who roguery scorns,
> And he gives me three farthings
> 　For poor cowly's horns.

This is better than our reading, and concludes thus:

> There's an end to my cowly,
> 　Now she's dead and gone;
> For the loss of my cowly
> 　I sob and I mourn.

A north of England song.

Says t' auld man tit oak-tree,
　Young and lusty was I when I kenn'd thee;
I was young and lusty, I was fair and clear,
　Young and lusty was I mony a lang year;
But sair fail'd am I, sair fail'd now,
　Sair fail'd am I sen I kenn'd thou.

My maid Mary she minds her dairy,
  While I go a-hoeing and mowing each morn;
Merrily run the reel and the little spinning-wheel
  Whilst I am singing and mowing my corn.

LITTLE Bo-peep has lost
    his sheep,
  And can't tell where to
    find them;
Leave them alone, and
    they'll come home,
  And bring their tails be-
    hind them.

Little Bo-peep fell fast asleep,
  And dreamt he heard them bleating;
But when he awoke he found it a joke,
  For they were all still fleeting.

Then up he took his little crook,
  Determined for to find them;
He found them indeed, but it made his heart bleed,
  For they'd left all their tails behind 'em!

WHEN I was a little boy
  I lived by myself;
And all the bread and
    cheese I got
  I put upon the shelf.

The rats and the mice
  They made such a strife,
I was forced to go to Lon-
    don town
  To buy me a wife.

The streets were so broad,
  And the lanes were so narrow,
I was forced to bring my wife home
  In a wheelbarrow.

The wheelbarrow broke,
  And my wife had a fall,
Down came wheelbarrow,
  Wife and all.

A PRETTY little girl in a round-
    eared cap
  I met in the streets t' other day;
She gave me such a thump,
  That my heart it went bump;
I thought I should have fainted
    away!
I thought I should have fainted
    away!

As I was going along, long, long,
A-singing a comical song, song,
    song,
The lane that I went was so long,
    long, long,
And the song that I sung was as
    long, long, long,
And so I went singing along.

The first line of this nursery rhyme is quoted in Beaumont and Fletcher's "Bonduca," Act V., sc. 2. It is probable also that Sir Toby alludes to this song in "Twelfth Night," Act II., sc. 2, when he says "Come on; there is sixpence for you: let's have a song." In "Epulario, or the Italian Banquet," 1589, is a receipt "to make pies so that the birds may be alive in them and flie out when it is cut up," —a mere device, live birds being introduced after the pie is made. This may be the original subject of the following song:

Sing a song of sixpence,
    A bag full of rye;
Four-and-twenty blackbirds
    Baked in a pie;
When the pie was opened
    The birds began to sing;
Was not that a dainty dish
    To set before the King?
The King was in his counting-house,
    Counting out his money;
The Queen was in the parlour,
    Eating bread and honey;
The maid was in the garden
    Hanging out the clothes;
By came a little bird,
    And snapt off her nose.

Jenny was so mad
    She didn't know what to do;
She put her finger in her ear,
    And cracked it right in two.

About the bush, Willy,
  About the bee-hive,
About the bush, Willy,
  I'll meet thee alive.

Then to my ten shillings
  Add you but a groat,
I'll go to Newcastle,
  And buy a new coat.

Five and five shillings,
  Five and a crown,
Five and five shillings
  Will buy a new gown.

Five and five shillings,
  Five and a groat;
Five and five shillings
  Will buy a new coat

From "Histrio-mastix; or, the Player Whipt," 4to, Lond. 1610. Mr. Rimbault says this is common in Yorkshire.

Some up and some down,
There's players in the town,
You wot well who they be
The sun doth arise
To three companies,
One, two, three, four, make we!

Besides we that travel,
With pumps full of gravel,
Made all of such running leather,
That once in a week
New masters we seek,
And never can hold together.

Old Father of the Pye,
I cannot sing, my lips are dry;
But when my lips are very well wet,
Then I can sing with the Heigh go Bet!

This appears to be an old hunting song. *Go bet* is a very ancient sporting phrase, equivalent to *go along.* It occurs in Chaucer.

As I was going up the hill,
  I met with Jack the piper,
And all the tunes that he could play
  Was "Tie up your petticoats tighter."
I tied them once, I tied them twice,
  I tied them three times over ;
And all the songs that he could sing
  Was "Carry me safe to Dover."

My father he died, but I can't tell you how,
He left me six horses to drive in my plough:
With my wing wang waddle oh,
Jack sing saddle oh,
Blowsey boys buble oh,
Under the broom.

I sold my six horses, and I bought me a cow,
I'd fain have made a fortune, but did not know how:
With my, &c.

I sold my cow, and I bought me a calf;
I'd fain have made a fortnne, but lost the best half:
With my, &c.

I sold my calf, and I bought me a cat;
A pretty thing she was, in my chimney corner sat:
With my, &c.

I sold my cat, and bought me a mouse;
He carried fire in his tail, and burnt down my house:
With my, &c.

THERE was a jolly miller
Lived on the River Dee;
He worked and sung from morn till night,
No lark so blithe as he;

And this the burden of his song
  For ever used to be—
I jump mejerrime jee!
  I care for nobody—no! not I,
Since nobody cares for me.

TRIP upon trenches, and
  dance upon dishes,
My mother sent me for
  some barm, some
  barm:
She bade me tread
  lightly, and come
  again quickly,
For fear the young men
  should do me some
  harm.
Yet didn't you see, yet
  didn't you see,
What naughty tricks they
  put upon me:

They broke my pitcher,
  And spilt the water,
And huffed my mother,
  And chid her daughter,
And kissed my sister instead of me.

IF I'd as much money as I could spend,
I never would cry old chairs to mend;
Old chairs to mend, old chairs to mend,
I never would cry old chairs to mend.

If I'd as much money as I could tell,
I never would cry old clothes to sell,
Old clothes to sell, old clothes to sell,
I never would cry old clothes to sell.

LONDON bridge is broken down,
Dance o'er my Lady Lee;
London bridge is broken down,
With a gay ladye.

How shall we build it up again?
Dance o'er my Lady Lee;
How shall we build it up again?
With a gay ladye.

Silver and gold will be stole away,
Dance o'er my Lady Lee;
Silver and gold will be stole away,
With a gay ladye.

Build it up again with iron and steel,
Dance o'er my Lady Lee;
Build it up with iron and steel,
With a gay ladye.

Iron and steel will bend and bow,
Dance o'er my Lady Lee;
Iron and steel will bend and bow,
With a gay ladye.

Build it up with wood and clay,
Dance o'er my Lady Lee;
Build it up with wood and clay,
With a gay ladye.

Wood and clay will wash away,
Dance o'er my Lady Lee;
Wood and clay will wash away,
With a gay ladye.

Build it up with stone so strong,
Dance o'er my Lady Lee;
Huzza ! t'will last for ages long,
With a gay ladye.

The following catch is found in Ben Jonson's "Masque of Oberon," and is a most common nursery song at the present day.

Buz, quoth the blue fly,
Hum, quoth the bee,
Buz and hum they cry,
And so do we:
In his ear, in his nose, thus, do you see ?
He ate the dormouse, else it was he.

Jacky, come give me the fiddle,
If ever thou mean to thrive,
Nay, I'll not give my fiddle
To any man alive.

If I should give my fiddle
They'll think that I'm gone mad,
For many a joyful day
My fiddle and I have had.

Johnny shall have a new bonnet,
And Johnny shall go to the fair,
And Johnny shall have a blue
ribbon
To tie up his bonny brown hair.
And why may not I love Johnny?
And why may not Johnny love
me?
And why may not I love Johnny,
As well as another body?

And here's a leg for a stocking,
And here is a leg for a shoe,
And he has a kiss for his daddy,
And two for his mammy, I trow.
And why may not I love Johnny?
And why may not Johnny love
me?
And why may not I love Johnny
As well as another body?

I love sixpence, pretty little sixpence,
I love sixpence better than my life;
I spent a penny of it, I spent another,
And took fourpence home to my wife.

Oh, my little fourpence, pretty little fourpence,
I love fourpence better than my life;
I spent a penny of it, I spent another,
And I took twopence home to my wife.

Oh, my little twopence, my pretty little twopence,
I love twopence better than my life;
I spent a penny of it, I spent another,
And I took nothing home to my wife.

Oh, my little nothing, my pretty little nothing,
　What will nothing buy for my wife?
I have nothing, I spend nothing,
　I love nothing better than my wife.

I HAVE been to market, my
　lady, my lady.
Then you've not been to the
　fair, says pussy, says pussy.
I bought me a rabbit, my
　lady, my lady.
Then you did not buy a hare,
　says pussy, says pussy.

I roasted it my lady,
　my lady.
Then you did not boil
　it, says pussy, says
　pussy.
I ate it, my lady, my
　lady.
And I'll eat you!
　says pussy.

My father left me three
　acres of land,
　Sing ivy, sing ivy;
My father left me three
　acres of land,
　Sing holly go whistle
　and ivy!

I ploughed it with a ram's
　horn,
　Sing ivy, sing ivy;
And sowed it all over with
　one peppercorn,
　Sing holly, go whistle
　and ivy!

I harrowed it with a bramble bush,
Sing ivy, sing ivy;
And reaped it with my little penknife,
Sing holly, go whistle, and ivy!

I got the mice to carry it to the barn,
Sing ivy, sing ivy;
And thrashed it with a goose's quill,
Sing holly, go whistle, and ivy!

I got the cat to carry it to the mill,
Sing ivy, sing ivy ;
The miller he swore he would have her paw,
And the cat she swore she would scratch his face,
Sing holly, go whistle, and ivy !

Wooley Foster has gone to sea,
With silver buckles at his knee,
When he comes back he'll marry me,
Bonny Wooley Foster !

Wooley Foster has a cow,
  Black and white about
  the mow,
Open the gates and let her
  through,
    Wooley Foster's ain
    cow !

Wooley Foster has a hen,
  Cockle button, cockle
  hen,
She lays eggs for gentle-
  men,
    But none for Wooley
    Foster !

Elsie Marley is said to have been a merry ale-wife who lived near
Chester, England, and the remainder of this song relating to her will be
found in the "Chester Garland." The first four lines have become
favorites in the nursery.

ELSIE MARLEY is grown so fine
She wont get up to serve the
  swine,
But lies in bed till eight or
  nine,
And surely she does take her
  time.
And do you ken Elsie Marley,
  honey ?
The wife who sells the barley,
  honey;
She won't get up to serve her
  swine,
And do you ken Elsie Marley,
  honey ?

THE north wind doth blow,
And we shall have snow,
And what will poor Robin
   do then?
      Poor thing!

He'll sit in a barn,
And to keep himself warm,
Will hide his head under his wing,
      Poor thing!

JOHN COOK had a little grey mare; he haw, hum!
Her back stood up, and her bones they were bare; he
   haw hum!

John Cook was riding up Shuter's bank; he haw, hum!
And there his nag did kick and prank; he, haw hum!

John Cook was riding up Shuter's hill; he haw, hum!
His mare fell down, and she made her will; he, haw,
   hum!

The bridle and saddle were laid on the shelf; he, haw,
   hum!

If you want any more you must sing it yourself; he,
   haw, hum!

Hot-cross Buns!
Hot-cross Buns!
One a penny, two a penny.
Hot-cross Buns!

Hot-cross Buns!
Hot-cross Buns!
If ye have no daughters
Give them to your sons.

The following lines are part of an old song, the whole of which may be found in "Deuteromelia," 1609, and also in MS. Additional, 5336, fol. 5.

OF all the gay birds
  that e'r I did see,
The owl is the fair-
  est by far to me ;
For all the day long
  she sits on a tree,
And when the night
  comes away flies
  she,
Te-wit, te-whou,
  Sir knave to thou,

This song is well sung, I make you a vow,
And he is a knave that drinketh not now.

SING song! merry go round,
  Here we go up to the moon, oh,
Little Johnnie a penny has found,
  And so we'll sing a tune, oh!
    What shall I buy?
    Johnnie did cry,
With the penny I, ve found
So bright and round?

What shall you buy?
A kite that will fly
Up to the moon, all
  through the sky!
But if, when it gets there,
It should stay in the air.
Or the man in the moon
Should open the door,
And take it in with his
  long, long paw,—
We should sing to another
  tune, oh!

The music to the following song, with different words, is given in "Melismata," 4to, Lond. 1611. See also the "Pills to Purge Melancholy," 1719, vol. i., p. 14. The well-known song, "A Frog he would a-wooing go," appears to have been borrowed from this. See Dauney's "Ancient Scottish Melodies," 1838, p. 53. The story is of old date, and in 1580 there was licensed "A most strange weddinge ot the frogge and the mouse," as appears from the books of the Stationers' Company quoted in Warton's Hist. Engl. Poet., ed. 1840, vol. iii, p. 360.

THERE was a frog lived in a well,
Kitty alone, Kitty alone;
There was a frog lived in a well;
Kitty alone and I!

There was a frog lived in a well;
And a farce* mouse in a mill,

Cock me carry, Kitty alone,
Kitty alone and I.

This frog he would a-wooing ride,
Kitty alone, &c.
This frog he would a-wooing ride,
And on a snail he got astride,
Cock me carry, &c.

*Merry.

He rode till he came to
my Lady Mouse Hall,
Kitty alone, &c.
He rode till he came to
my Lady Mouse Hall,
And there he did both
knock and call,
Cock me carry, &c.

Quoth he, "Miss Mouse,
I'm come to thee,"—
Kitty alone, &c.
Quoth he, "Miss Mouse,
I'm come to thee,
To see if thou canst fancy
me."
Cock me carry, &c.

Quoth she, "Answer
I'll give you
none"—
Kitty alone, &c.
Quoth she, "Answer I'll
give you none
Until my Uncle Rat come
home."
Cock me carry, &c.

And when her Uncle Rat
came home,
Kitty alone, &c.
And when her Uncle Rat
came home:
"Who's been here since
I've been gone?"
Cock me carry, &c.

"Sir there's been a worthy
gentleman"—
Kitty alone, &c.
"Sir there's been a worthy
gentleman—
That's been here since
you've been gone."
Cock me carry, &c.

The frog he came whistling
through the brook,
Kitty alone, &c.
The frog he came whist-
ling through the
brook,
And there he met with
a dainty duck.
Cock me carry, &c.

This duck she swallowed him up with a pluck,
Kitty alone, Kitty alone;
This duck she swallowed him up with a pluck
So there's an end of my history-book.
Cock me carry, Kitty alone,
Kitty alone and I.

Part of this is in a song called "Jockey's Lamentation," in the "Pills to Purge Melancholy," 1719, vol. v, p. 317.

TOM he was a piper's son,
He learned to play when he was young,
But all the tunes that he could play,
Was "Over the hills and far away,"
Over the hills and a great way off,
And the wind will blow my top-knot off.

Now, Tom with his pipe made such a noise,
That he pleased both the girls and boys,
And they stopped to hear him play
"Over the hills and far away."

Tom with his pipe did play with such skill,
That those who heard him could never keep still;
Whenever they heard they began for to dance,—
Even pigs on their hind legs would after him prance.

As Dolly was milking her cow one day,
Tom took out his pipe and began for to play;
So Doll and the cow danced "the Cheshire round,"
Till the pail was broke, and the milk ran on the ground.

He met old Dame Trot with a basket of eggs,
He used his pipe and she used her legs;
She danced about till the eggs were all broke,
She began for to fret, but he laughed at the joke.

He saw a cross fellow was beating an ass,
Heavy laden with pots, pans, dishes and glass;

He took out his pipe and played them a tune,
And the jackass's load was lightened full soon.

MERRY are the bells, and merry would they ring,
Merry was myself, and merry could I sing;
With a merry ding-dong, happy, gay, and free,
And a merry sing-song, happy let us be!

Waddle goes your gait, and hollow are your hose,
Noddle goes your pate, and purple is your nose;
Merry is your sing-song, happy, gay, and free,
With a merry ding-dong, happy let us be!

Merry have we met, and merry have we been,
Merry let us part, and merry meet again;
With our merry sing-song, happy, gay, and free,
And a merry ding-dong, happy let us be!

WHAT is your father, my pretty maid?
My father's a farmer, sir, she said
Say, will you marry me, my pretty maid?
Yes, if you please, kind sir, she said.

Will you be constant, my pretty maid?
That I can't promise you, sir, she said.
Then I won't marry you, my pretty maid;
Nobody asked you sir! she said.

A CARRION crow sat on an oak,
    Fol de riddle, lol de riddle, hi ding do,
Watching a tailor shape his cloak.
    Sing heigh ho, the carrion crow,
      Fol de riddle, lol de riddle, hi ding do.

Wife, bring me my old bent bow,
   Fol de riddle, lol de riddle, hi ding do,
That I may shoot yon carrion crow.
   Sing heigh ho, &c.

The tailor he shot and missed his mark,
   Fol de riddle, lol de riddle, hi ding do,
And shot his own sow quite to the heart;
   Sing heigh ho, &c.

Wife, bring brandy in a spoon;
   Fol de riddle, lol de riddle, hi ding do,
For our old sow is in a swoon,
   Sing heigh ho, the carrion crow,
   Fol de riddle, lol de riddle, di ding do.

Another version from MS. Sloane, 1489, fol. 17, written in the time of Charles I.

Hic hoc, the carrion crow,
For I have shot something too low;
I have quite missed my mark,
And shot the poor sow to the heart;
Wife, bring treacle in a spoon,
Or else the poor sow's heart will down.

THERE were two birds
    sat on a stone,
Fa, la, la, la, lal, de;
One flew away, and
    then there was one,
Fa, la, la, la, lal, de;

The other flew after, and
    then there was none,
Fa, la, la, la, lal de;
And so the poor stone
    was left all alone,
Fa, la, la, la, lal, de!

Of these two birds one
    back again flew,
Fa, la, la, la, lal, de;
The other came after,
    and then there were two,
Fa, la, la, la, lal, de;

Said one to the other,
    "Pray how do you do?"
Fa, la, la, la, lal, de;
"Very well, thank you,
    and pray how do you?"
Fa, la, la, la, lal, de!

[Song of a little boy while passing his hour of solitude in a cornfield.]

Away, birds, away,
Take a little, and leave
    a little,
And do not come again;

For if you do,
I will shoot you through,
And there is an end
    of you.

There were three jovial
    huntsmen,
    As I have heard them
    say,
And they would go a-
    hunting
All on a summer's day.

All the day they hunted,
    And nothing could they
    find
But a ship a-sailing,
    A-sailing with the wind.
One said it was a ship,
    The other said Nay;

The third said it was a
    house
    With the chimney blown
    away.

And all the night they
    hunted,
    And nothing could they
    find;
But the moon a-gliding,
    A-gliding with the wind.
One said it was the moon,
    The other said Nay;
The third said it was a
    cheese,
And half o't cut away.

DAME, get up and bake your pies,
   Bake your pies, bake your pies,
Dame, get up and bake your pies
   On Christmas Day in the morning.

Dame, what makes your maidens lie,
   Maidens lie, maidens lie,
Dame, what makes your maidens lie
   On Christmas Day in the morning?

Dame, what makes your ducks to die,
   Ducks to die, ducks to die,
Dame, what makes your ducks to die
   On Christmas day in the morning.

How does my
  lady's garden
    grow?
How does my
  lady's garden
    grow?
With cockle-
  shells and
   silver bells,
And pretty
  maids all
   of a row.

A FROG he would a-wooing go,
          Heigho, says Rowley,
Whether his mother would let him or no.
    With a rowley powley, gammon and spinach,
    Heigho, says Anthony Rowley.

So off he set with his opera hat,
          Heigho, says Rowley.
And on the road he met with a rat.
          With a rowley, powley, &c.

"Pray, Mr. Rat, will you go with me,
>> Heigho, says Rowley,
Kind Mrs. Mousey for to see?"
>> With a rowley powley, &c.

When they came to the door of Mousey's hall,
>> Heigho, says Rowley,
They gave a loud knock and they gave a loud call.
>> With a rowley powley, &c.

"Pray, Mrs. Mouse, are you within?"
>> Heigho, says Rowley,
"Oh, yes, kind sirs, I'm sitting to spin."
>> With a rowley powley, &c.

"Pray, Mrs. Mouse, will you give us some beer?
>> Heigho, says Rowley,
For Froggy and I are fond of good cheer."
>> With a rowley powley, &c.

"Pray, Mr. Frog, will you give us a song?
>> Heigho, says Rowley,
But let it be something that's not very long."
>> With a rowley powley, &c.

"Indeed, Mrs. Mouse," replied the frog,
>> Heigho, says Rowley,
"A cold has made me as hoarse as a dog."
>> With a rowley powley, &c.

"Since you have caught cold, Mr. Frog," Mousey said,
>> Heigho, says Rowley,
"I'll sing you a song that I have just made."
>> With a rowley powley, &c.

But while they were all a merry-making,
>> Heigho, says Rowley,
A cat and her kittens came tumbling in
>> With a rowley powley, &c.

The cat she seized the rat by the crown;

Heigho, says Rowley.

The kittens they pulled the little mouse down.

With a rowley powley, &c.

This put Mr. Frog in a terrible fright,

Heigho, says Rowley,

He took up his hat, and he wished them good night.

With a rowley powley, &c.

But as Froggy was crossing over a brook,

Heigho, says Rowley,

A lily-white duck came and gobbled him up.

With a rowley powley, &c.

So there was an end of one, two, and three,

Heigho, says Rowley,

The Rat, the Mouse, and the little Frog-gee!

With a rowley powley, gammon and spinach

Heigho, says Anthony Rowley.

WHISTLE, daughter, whistle; whistle, daughter, dear.
I cannot whistle, mamma, I cannot whistle clear.
Whistle, daughter, whistle; whistle for a pound.
I cannot whistle, mammy, I cannot make a sound.

Song on the bells of Derby, England, on foot-ball morning, a custom now discontinued.

PANCAKES and fritters,
  Say All Saints and St.
    Peters;
When will the BALL come?
  Say the bells of St. Alk-
    mun;

At two they will throw,
Says Saint Werabo,
Oh, very well,
Says little Michel.

I'LL sing you a song,
  Though not very long,
Yet I think it as pretty as
    any;

Put your hand in your
  purse,
You'll never be worse,
And give the poor singer
  a penny.

THE miller he grinds his corn, his corn;
The miller he grinds his corn, his corn;
The little boy blue comes winding his horn,
    With a hop, step, and a jump.

The carter he whistles aside his team;
The carter he whistles aside his team;
And Dolly comes tripping with the nice clouted cream,
    With a hop, step, and a jump.

The nightingale sings when we're at rest;
The nightingale sings when we're at rest;
The little bird climbs the tree for his nest,
    With a hop, step, and a jump.

The damsels are churning for curds and whey;
The damsels are churning for curds and whey:
The lads in the field are making the hay,
    With a hop, step, and a jump.

THERE was a man in our toone, in our toone, in our toone,
There was a man in our toone, and his name was Billy
    Pod;
And he played upon an old razor, an old razor, an old
    razor,
And he played upon an old razor, with my fiddle fiddle
    fe fum fo.

And his hat it was made of the good roast beef, the
    good roast beef, the good roast beef,
And his hat was made of the good roast beef, and his
    name was Billy Pod;
And he played upon an old razor, &c.

And his coat it was made of the good fat tripe, the
    good fat tripe, the good fat tripe,
And his coat it was made of the good fat tripe, and his
    name was Billy Pod;
And he played upon an old razor, &c.

And his breeks were made of the bawbie baps, the
    bawbie baps, the bawbie baps,
And his breeks were made of the bawbie baps, and his
    name was Billy Pod;
And he played upon an old razor, &c.

And there was a man in tither toone, in tither toone, in
    tither toone,
And there was a man in tither toone, and his name was
    Edrin Drum;
And he played upon an old laadle, an old laadle, an old
    laadle,
And he played upon an old laadle, with my fiddle fiddle
    fe fum fo.

And he ate up all the good roast beef, the good roast
    beef, &c.
And he ate up all the good fat tripe, the good fat
    tripe, &c.
And he ate up all the bawbie baps, &c., and his name
    was Edrin Drum.

I saw three ships come sailing by,
    Come sailing by, come sailing by—
I saw three ships come sailing by,
    New Year's Day in the morning.

And what do you think was in them then,
    Was in them then, was in them then?
And what do you think was in them then?
    New Year's Day in the morning.

Three pretty girls were in them then,
    Were in them then, were in them then—
Three pretty girls were in them then,
    New Year's Day in the morning.

One could whistle, and another could sing,
    And the other could play on the violin—

Such joy was there at my wedding,
New Year's Day in the morning.

OH, who is so merry, so
merry, heigh ho!
As the light-hearted fairy,
heigh ho, heigh ho!
He dances and sings
To the sound of his
wings,
With a hey, and a heigh,
and a ho!

Oh, who is so merry, so
airy, heigh ho!
As the light-headed fairy,
heigh ho, heigh ho!
His nectar he sips
From the primrose's lips,
With a hey, and a heigh,
and a ho!

Oh, who is so merry, so merry, heigh ho!
As the light-footed fairy, heigh ho, heigh ho!
His night is the noon,
And his sun is the moon,
With a hey, and a heigh, and a ho!

As I was going to Derby all on a market-day,
I met the finest ram, sir, that ever was fed upon hay;
Upon hay, upon hay, upon hay;
I met the finest ram, sir, that ever was fed upon hay.

This ram was fat behind, sir; this ram was fat before;
This ram was ten yards round, sir; indeed he was no more.
No more, no more, no more;
This ram was ten yards round, sir; indeed he was no more.

The horns that grew on his head, sir, they were so
wondrous high,
As I've been plainly told, sir, they reached up to the sky.
The sky, the sky, the sky;
As I've been plainly told, sir, they reached up to the sky.

The tail that grew from his back, sir, was six yards and
an ell;
And it was sent to Derby to toll the market bell;
The bell, the bell, the bell;
And it was sent to Derby to toll the market bell.

I WILL sing you a song,
Though it is not very long,
Of the woodcock and the sparrow,
Of the little dog that burned his
tail,
And the boy that must be whipt
to-morrow.

Riddles.

THERE was a girl in our towne,
Silk an' satin was her gowne,
Silk an' satin, gold an' velvet,
Guess her name—three times I've tell'd it.   Ann.

RIDDLE-ME, riddle-me, riddle-me-ree,
Perhaps you can tell what this riddle may be:
As deep as a house, as round as a cup,
And all the King's horses can't draw it up.

A well.

I WENT to the wood and got it,
I sat me down and looked at it;
The more I looked at it the less I liked it,
And brought it home because I couldn't help it.

A thorn.

I'M in every one's way,   My four horns every day
  But no one I stop;   In every way play,
        And my head is nailed on at the top.

A turnstile.

THE cuckoo and the gowk,
The laverock and the lark,
The twire-snipe, the weather-bleak,
How many birds is that?

Three, for the second name in each line is a synonym.

[The cuckoo is called a *gowk* in the north of England; the lark, a
laverock ; and the twire-snipe and weather-bleak, or weather-bleater,
are the same birds.]

HODDY-DODDY,
With a round black body;
Three feet and a wooden hat:
What's that ?   An iron pot.

An iron pot with three legs, and a wooden cover, the latter raised or
put on by means of a peg at the top, is used for suspending over a fire,
or to place on the hearth with a wood fire.

THE fiddler and his wife,
    The piper and his mother,
Ate three half cakes, three whole cakes,
    And three quarters of another:
How much did each get ?

The fiddler's wife was the piper's mother.   Each one
therefore got $\frac{1}{2} + 1 + \frac{1}{4}$ or $1\frac{3}{4}$.

RIDDLE me, riddle me, what is that,
Over the head and under the hat ?   Hair.
                [From Kent.]

THERE was a little green house
And in the little green house
There was a little brown house,
And in the little brown house
There was a little yellow house,
And in the little yellow house
There was a little white house,
And in the little white house
There was a little heart.
                                A walnut.

A FLOCK of white sheep   Here they go, there they go,
On a red hill;   Now they stand still!
                                The teeth and gums.

As I was going o'er London Bridge,
I met a cart full of fingers and thumbs!
                                Gloves.

Lives in winter,   Dies in summer,
   And grows with its root upwards!

                                   An icicle.

Old father Greybeard,   If you'll give me your finger,
Without tooth or tongue,   I'll give you my thumb.

When I went up sandy hill,
   I met a sandy boy;
I cut his throat, I sucked his blood,
   And left his skin a-hanging-o.

As I was going o'er London Bridge,
   And peeped through a nick,
I saw four-and-twenty ladies
   Riding on a stick!

                  A firebrand with sparks on it.

I have a little sister, they call her peep, peep;
She wades the waters deep, deep, deep;
She climbs the mountains high, high, high;
Poor little creature! she has but one eye.

                             A star.

Hick-a-more, Hack-a-more,
On the King's kitchen-door;
All the King's horses,
And all the King's men,
Couldn't drive Hick-a-more, Hack-a-more,
Off the King's kitchen-door!

                            Sunshine.

Old Mother Twitchett had but one eye,
And a long tail which she let fly;
And every time she went over a gap,
She left a bit of her tail in a trap.

                        A needle and thread.

WHAT shoemaker makes shoes without leather,
With all the four elements put together?
    Fire and water, earth and air;
    Every customer has two pair.

                                A horse-shoer.

I WENT into my grandmother's garden,
And there I found a farthing.
I went into my next-door neighbor's,
There I bought a pipkin and a popkin,
   A slipkin and a slopkin,
   A nailboard, a sailboard,
   And all for a farthing.   A pipe.

MADE in London,   Stops a bottle,
Sold at York,   And *is* a cork.

The allusion to Öliver Cromwell satisfactorily fixes the date of the riddle
to belong to the seventeenth century.   The answer is, a rainbow.

PURPLE, yellow, red, and green,
The King cannot reach it, nor the Queen;
Nor can old Noll, whose power's so great;
Tell me this riddle while I count eight.

    HIGGEDLY piggeldy
      Here we lie,
    Picked and plucked,
      And put in a pie.
My first is snapping, snarling, growl-
    ing,
My second's industrious, romping, and
    prowling.
    Higgeldy piggeldy
      Here we lie,
    Picked and plucked,
      And put in a pie.   Currants.

As I looked out of my chamber window
   I heard something fall;
I sent my maid to pick it up,
   But she couldn't pick it all.   Snuff.

HUMPTY DUMPTY sat on a wall,
Humpty Dumpty had a great fall,
Threescore men and threescore more
Cannot place Humpty Dumpty as he was before.

An Egg.

BLACK we are, but much
  admired;
Men seek for us till they are
  tired.
We tie the horse, but com-
  fort man:
Tell me this riddle if you
  can.   Coal.

THOMAS A TATTAMUS took
  two Ts
To tie two tups to two tall
  trees,
To frighten the t e r r i b l e
  Thomas a Tattamus!
Tell me how many Ts there
  are in all THAT ?

WHEN I was taken from the fair body,
  They then cut off my head,
  And thus my shape was altered.
It's I that make peace between King and King,
  And many a true lover glad:
All this I do, and ten times more,
  And more I could do still ;
But nothing can I do
  Without my guider's will.   A pen.

ARTHUR O'BOWER has broken his band;
He comes roaring up the land.
The King of Scots with all his power,
Cannot turn Arthur of the Bower!
                    A storm of wind.

THE calf, the goose, the bee,
The world is ruled by these three.
            Parchment, pens, and wax.

TWELVE pears hanging high,
Twelve knights riding by;
Each knight took a pear,
And yet left eleven there!

WHAT GOD never sees,
What the King seldom sees,
What we may every day:
Read my riddle, I pray.
                          An Equal.

THE land was white,
The seed was black;
It'll take a good scholar
To riddle me that.
                          Paper and writing.

As high as a castle,
As weak as a wastle;
And all the King's horses
Cannot pull it down.
                          Smoke.

A wastle is a North of England term for a twig or withy, possibly connected with A. S. *wædl*.

As white as milk
And not milk;
As green as grass
And not grass,
As red as blood,
And not blood;
As black as soot,
And not soot!
                          A bramble blossom.

A young man and a young woman quarrelled, and the former, in his anger, exclaimed,

Three words I know to be true,
All which begin with W.

The young woman immediately guessed the enigma, and replied in a similiar strain,

I too know them,
And eke three which begin with M.

Woman Wants Wit. Man Much More.

Banks full, braes full,
 Though ye gather all day,
Ye'll not gather your hands full. The mist.

From Northumberland, England.—Sometimes thus:

A hill full, a hole full,
Ye cannot catch a bowlful.

In marble walls as white as milk,
Lined with a skin as soft as silk,
Within a fountain crystal clear
A golden apple doth appear.
No doors there are to this stronghold,
Yet thieves break in and steal the gold.

I've seen you where you never was,
 And where you ne'er will be,
And yet you in that very same place
 May still be seen by me.
 The reflection of a face in a looking-glass.

Make three-fourths of a
 cross,
 And a circle complete;
And let two semicircles
 On a perpendicular
   meet;

Next add a triangle
 That stands on two feet;
Next two semicircles,
 And a circle complete.
   Tobacco.

THERE was a King met a King
In a narrow lane,
Says this King to that King,
"Where have you been?"

"Oh! I've been a-hunting
With my dog and my doe."
"Pray lend him to me,
That I may do so,"

"There's the dog, *take* the dog."
"What's the dog's name?"
"I've told you already."
"Pray tell me again."

FLOUR of England, fruit of Spain,
Met together in a shower of rain;
Put in a bag tied round with a string:
If you'll tell me this riddle, I'll give you a ring.

A plum pudding.

As I was going o'er yon moor of moss,
I met a man on a grey horse;
He whipped and he wailed;
I asked him what he ailed;
He said he was going to his father's funeral,
Who died seven years before he was born!

His father was a dyer.

As I was going o'er London Bridge
I met a drove of guinea pigs;
They were nicked and they were nacked,
And they were all yellow backed.

A swarm of bees.

Not a very likely family to meet in that neighborhood, at least now-
adays; but some of the authors of these poems seem to have been con-
tinually traversing London Bridge.

Which weighs heavier—   Or a stone of feather?
  A stone of lead   They both weigh alike.

LILLYLOW, lillylow, set up on an end,
See little baby go out at town end.

A candle.

"Lillylow" is a North of England term for the flame of a candle. Low
A.S. *lig*, is universal.

AT the end of my yard there is a vat,—
Four-and-twenty ladies dancing in that;
Some in green gowns, and some with blue hat:
He is a wise man who can tell me that.

A field of flax.

THERE was a man went over the Wash,
Grizzle grey was his horse;
Bent was his saddle-bow:
I've told you his name three times,
And yet you don't know!   Gaffer Was.

I AM become of flesh and blood,
  As other creatures be;
Yet there's neither flesh nor blood
  Doth remain in me.
I make Kings that they fall out:
  I make them agree;
And yet there's neither flesh nor blood
  Doth remain in me.   A pen.

BLACK'M, saut'm, rough'm glower'm saw,
Click'm, gatt'm, flaug'm into girnigaw.
Eating a sloe.

A North of England riddle, given by Brockett. "Girnigaw" is the cavity of the mouth.

INTO my house came neighbor John,
With three legs and a wooden one;
If one be taken from the same,
Then just five there will remain.

He had a IV-legged stool with him, and taking away the left-hand numeral, there remains V.

JACKATAWAD ran over the moor:
Never behind, but always before!
The *ignis fatuus*, or Will-o'-the-wisp.

"Jackatawad" is an English provincial term for this phenomenon.

LINK lank on a bank,
Ten against four.   A milkmaid.

Two legs sat upon three legs,
With four legs standing by;
Four then were drawn by ten:
Read my riddle ye can't,
However much ye try.

An amplification of the above, the milkmaid, of course, sitting on a three-legged stool.

As straight as a maypole,   As bent as a bucker,
As little as a pin,   And as round as a ring.

We do not know the solution of this riddle. A "bucker" is a bent piece of wood by which slaughtered sheep are hung up by their expanded hind legs, before being cut out.

Over the water,
And under the water,
And always with its head down.

A nail in the bottom of a ship.

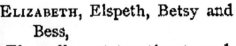

Elizabeth, Elspeth, Betsy and
  Bess,
They all went together to seek
  a bird's nest.
They found a bird's nest with
  five eggs in,
They all took one, and left four
  in.

Every lady in this land
Has twenty nails upon each
  hand,
Five and twenty hands and
  feet:
All this is true without deceit.

Long legs, crooked thighs,
Little head, and no eyes.

Pair of tongs.

A house full, a yard full,
And ye can't catch a bowl full.

Smoke.

Thirty white horses upon a red hill,
Now they tramp, now they champ, now they stand still.

Teeth and gums.

The moon nine days old,
The next sign to Cancer,
Pat, rat without a tail;—

And now, sir, for your
answer.

C-leo-pat-ra.

From MS. Sloane, 1489, fol. 16, written in the time of Charles I.

THERE were three sisters in a hall,
There came a knight amongst them all;
Good morrow, aunt, to the one,
Good morrow, aunt, to the other,
Good morrow, gentlewoman, to the third:
If you were my aunt, as the other two be,
I would say good morrow, then aunts all three.

CONGEALED water and Cain's brother,
That was my lover's name, and no other.　　Isabel.

BLACK within and red　Four corners round about.
without　　　　　　　　　　　　　A chimney.

THERE was a man rode through our town,
　Gray Grizzle was his name;
His saddle-bow was gilt with gold:
　Three times I've named his name.

PEASE-PORRIDGE hot, pease-porridge cold,
Pease-porridge in the pot, nine days old.
Spell me *that* without a P,
And a clever scholar you will be.

A RIDDLE, a riddle, as I suppose,
A hundred eyes, and never a nose.　A cinder-sifter.

As round as an apple, as deep as a cup,
And all the King's horses can't pull it up.　　A well.

As I went through the garden gap,
　Who should I meet but Dick Red-cap!
A stick in his hand, a stone in his throat:
If you'll tell me this riddle, I'll give you a groat.
　　　　　　　　　　　　　　　A cherry.

LITTLE Nancy Etticoat,
In a white petticoat,
And a red nose;

The longer she stands,
The shorter she grows.

As I was going o'er Westminster Bridge,
I met with a Westminster scholar;
He pulled off his cap *an' drew* off his glove,
And wished me a very good morrow
What is his name?

THERE was a man who had no eyes,
He went abroad to view the skies;
He saw a tree with apples on it,
He took no apples off, yet left no apples on it,
The man had one eye, and the
tree two apples upon it.

As I went over Lincoln Bridge,
I met Mister Rusticap;
Pins and needles on his back,
A going to Thorney fair.   A hedgehog.

FORMED long ago, yet made to-day
Employed while others sleep;
What few would like to give away,
Nor any wish to keep.   A bed.

THE first letter of our fore-fadyr,
A worker of wax,
An I and an N;
The color of an ass;
And what have you then?
A-b-in-dun, or Abingdon, in Berks, England.
An ancient rebus given in *Lelandi Itin.*, ed. 1744, ii. 136.

HIGHER than a house, higher than a tree;
Oh, whatever can that be?   A star.

Two legs sat upon
   three legs,
With one leg in his
   lap;
In comes four legs,
And runs away with
   one leg.
Up jumps two legs,
Catches up three legs,
Throws it after four
   legs,
And makes him bring
   back one leg.

One leg is a leg of mutton; two legs, a man; three
legs, a stool; four legs, a dog.

As I was going to St. Ives,
I met a man with seven wives,
Every wife had seven sacks,
Every sack had seven cats,
Every cat had seven kits:
Kits, cats, sacks, and wives,
How many were there going to St. Ives?

SEE, see, what shall I see?
A horse's head where his tail should be.

HITTY PITTY within the wall,
Hitty Pitty without the wall:
If you touch Hitty Pitty,
Hitty Pitty will bite you.   A nettle.

MS. Harl. 1962, xvii. cent.

I saw a fight the other day:
A damsel did begin the fray.
She with her daily friend did meet,
Then standing in the open street;
She gave such hard and sturdy blows,
He bled ten gallons at the nose;
Yet neither seem to faint nor fall,
Nor gave her any abuse at all.　　　　A pump.

MS. Harl. 1962, xvii. cent.

A water there is I must pass,
A broader water never was;
And yet of all waters I ever did see,
　To pass over with less jeopardy.　　　The dew.

From the same MS.

As I went over Hottery Tottery,
I looked into Horbora Lilly;
I spied a cutterell
Playing with her cambril,
I cryed, Ho, neighbor, ho!
Lend me your cue and your goe,
To shoot at yonder cutterell
Playing with her cambril,
And you shall have the curle of her loe.
A man calling to his neighbor for a gun to shoot a
deer, and he should have her humbles.

There is a bird of great renown,
Useful in city and in town;
None work like unto him can do;
He's yellow, black, red, and green,
A very pretty bird I mean;
Yet he's both fierce and fell:
I count him wise that can this tell.　　A bee.

MS. Harl. 1962, xvii. cent.

I HAVE four sisters beyond the sea,
    Para-mara, dictum, domine.
And they did send four presents to me,
    Partum, quartum, paradise, tempum,
    Para-mara, dictum, domine!

The first it was a bird without e'er a bone;
    Para-mara, dictum, &c.
The second was a cherry without e'er a stone;
    Partum, quartum, &c.

The third it was a blanket without e'er a thread,
    Para-mara, dictum, &c.
The fourth it was a book which no man could read,
    Partum, quartum, &c.

How can there be a bird without e'er a bone?
    Para-mara, dictum, &c.
How can there be a cherry without e'er a stone?
    Partum, quartum, &c.

How can there be a blanket without e'er a thread?
    Para-mara, dictum, &c.
How can there be a book which no man can read?
    Partum, quartum, &c.

When the bird's in the shell, there is no bone;
    Para-mara, dictum, &c.
When the cherry's in the bud, there is no stone;
    Partum, quartum, &c.

When the blanket's in the fleece, there is no thread;
    Para-mara, dictum, &c.
When the book's in the press, no man can read;
    Partum, quartum, &c.

Several versions of this metrical riddle are common in the north of England.

As I went through my houter touter,
   Houter trouter, verily;
I see one Mr. Higamgige
   Come over the hill of Parley.
But if I had my carly verly,
   Carly verly verly,
I would have bine met with Higamgige
   Come over the hill of Parley.
A man going over a hill, and a fly lighting on his head.

HIGHTY, tighty, paradighty clothed in green,
The King could not read it, no more could the Queen;
They sent for a wise man out of the East,
Who said it had horns, but was not a beast!
                           The Holly Tree.

I HAD a little castle upon the sea-sand,
   One-half was water, the other was land;
I opened my little castle door, and guess what I found:
   I found a fair lady with a cup in her hand.
   The cup was gold, filled with wine;
   Drink, fair lady, and thou shalt be mine!

As I was going o'er Tipple Tine,
I met a flock of bonny swine;
   Some green-lapped, some green-backed;
They were the very bonniest swine
That e'er went over Tipple Tine.
                    A swarm of bees.

   TEN and ten and twice eleven,
   Take out six and put in seven;
   Go to the green and fetch eighteen,
   And drop one a-coming.

As soft as silk, as white as milk,
As bitter as gall, a thick wall,
And a green coat covers me all.

A walnut.

———

HUMPTY DUMPTY lay in a beck*
With all his sinews round his neck;
Forty doctors and forty wrights
Couldn't put Humpty Dumpty to rights!

An egg.

* A brook.

EIGHTH CLASS.

Charms.

The following, with a very slight variation, is found in Ben Jonson's "Masque of Queen's," and it is singular to account for its introduction into the modern nursery.

I WENT to the toad that lies under the wall,
I charmed him out, and he came at my call;
I scratched out the eyes of the owl before,
I tore the bat's wing: what would you have more?

CUSHY cow bonny, let down thy milk,
And I will give thee a gown of silk;
A gown of silk and a silver tee,
If thou wilt let down thy milk to me.

Ady, in his "Candle in the Dark," 4to, Lond. 1656. p. 59, says that this was a charm to make butter come from the churn. It was to be said thrice.

Come, butter, come,
Come, butter, come!
Peter stands at the gate,

Waiting for a buttered cake;
Come, butter, come!

From Dr. Wallis's "Grammatica Linguæ Anglicanæ," 12mo, Oxon. 1674. p. 164. This and various others are said to be certain cures for the hiccup if repeated in one breath.

When a Twister a-twisting, will twist him a twist;
For the twisting of his twist, he three times doth intwist;
But if one of the twines of the twist do untwist,
The twine that untwisteth, unwisteth the twist.

Untwirling the twine that untwisteth between,
He twirls with the twister, the two in a twine:
Then twice having twisted the twines of the twine,
He twisteth the twine he had twined in twain.

The twain that, in twining, before in the twine
As twines were intwisted, he now doth untwine:
'Twixt the twain intertwisting a twine more between,
He, twirling his twister, makes a twist of the twine.

A thatcher of Thatchwood went to Thatchet a-thatch
  ing;
Did a thatcher of Thatchwood go to Thatchet a-thatch-
  ing?
If a thatcher of Thatchwood went to Thatchet a-thatch-
  ing,
Where's the thatching the thatcher of Thatchwood has
  thatched?

Sometimes "off a pewter plate" is added at the end of each line.

Peter Piper picked a peck of pickled pepper;
A peck of pickled pepper Peter Piper picked;
If Peter Piper picked a peck of pickled pepper,
Where's the peck of pickled pepper Peter Piper picked?

SWAN swam over the sea   Swan swam back again,
  Swim, swan, swim;   Well swum, swan.

THREE crooked cripples went through Cripplegate, and
  through Cripplegate went three crooked cripples.

ROBERT ROWLEY rolled a round roll round,
A round roll Robert Rowley rolled round;
Where rolled the round roll Robert Rowley rolled
  round?

Said to pips placed in the fire; a species of divination practised by children.

      IF you love me, pop and fly;
      If you hate me, lay and die.

  My grandmother sent me a new-fashioned three-
cornered cambric country-cut handkerchief. Not an
old-fashioned three-cornered cambric country-cut handkerchief, but a new-fashioned three-cornered cambric
country-cut handkerchief.

HICKUP, snicup,   Three drops in the cup
Rise up, right up!   Are good for the hiccup.

     HICKUP, hickup, go away!
     Come again another day;
     Hickup, hickup, when I bake,
     I'll give to you a butter-cake.

A charm somewhat similar to the following may be seen in the "Townley Mysteries," p. 91. See a paper in the "Archæologia," vol. xxvii. p. 253, by the Rev. Lancelot Sharpe, M.A. See also MS. Lansd. 231, fol. 114, and "Ady's Candle in the Dark," 4to, London, 1650, p. 58.

MATTHEW, Mark, Luke, and John,
Guard the bed that I lie on!
Four corners to my bed;
Four angels round my head,
One to watch, one to pray,
And two to bear my soul away!

My father he left me, just as he was able,
One bowl, one bottle, one label,
Two bowls, two bottles, two labels,
Three, &c. [*And so on ad lib. in one breath.*]

NINTH CLASS.

Gaffers and Gammers.

THERE was an old woman, as I've heard tell,
She went to market her eggs for to sell;
She went to market all on a market day,
And she fell asleep on the King's highway.

There came by a pedlar, whose name was Stout,—
He cut her petticoats all round about;
He cut her petticoats up to the knees,
Which made the old woman to shiver and freeze.

When this little woman first did wake,
She began to shiver and she began to shake,

She began to wonder and she began to cry,
" Oh! deary, deary me, this is none of I!

" But if it be I, as I do hope it be,
I have a little dog at home, and he'll know me;
If it be I, he'll wag his little tail,
And if it be not I, he'll loudly bark and wail."

Home went the little woman all in the dark:
Up got the little dog, and he began to bark;
He began to bark, so she began to cry,
" Oh! deary, deary me, this is none of I!"

THERE was an old man of Tobago,
Who lived on rice, gruel, and sago;
Till, much to his bliss,
His physician said this—
" To a leg, sir, of mutton you may go."

OLD mother Hubbard
Went to the cupboard
To get her poor dog a bone;
But when she came there,
The cupboard was bare,
And so the poor dog had none.

She went to the baker's
　To buy him some bread,
But when she came back
　The poor dog was dead.

She went to the joiner's
　To buy him a coffin,

But when she came back
The poor dog was laughing.*

She took a clean dish
To get him some tripe,
But when she came back
He was smoking his pipe.

She went to the fishmonger's
To buy him some fish,
And when she came back
He was licking the dish.

She went to the fruiterer's
To buy him some fruit,
But when she came back
He was playing the flute.

She went to the ale-house
To get him some beer,
But when she came back
The dog sat in a chair.

* Probably *loffing* or *loffin'*, to complete the rhyme.   So in Shakespeare's
" Midsummer Night's Dream," Act II., sc. 1.
" And then the whole quire hold their hips, and *loffe*."

She went to the hatter's
 To buy him a hat,
But when she came back
 He was feeding the cat.

She went to the barber's
 To buy him a wig,
But when she came back
 He was dancing a jig.

She went to the tavern
 For white wine and red,
But when she came back
 The dog stood on his head.

She went to the sempstress
  To buy him some linen,
But when she came back
  The dog was spinning.

She went to the tailor's
  To buy him a coat,
But when she came back
  He was riding a goat.

She went to the cobbler's
  To buy him some shoes,
But when she came back
  He was reading the news.

She went to the
hosier's
To buy him some
hose,
But when she came
back
He was dressed in
his clothes.

The dame made a curtsey,
The dog made a bow;
The dame said, "Your servant;".
The dog said, "Bow, wow."

A LITTLE old man of Derby,
How do you think he served me?
He took away my bread and cheese,
And that is how he served me.

THERE was an old woman
   Lived under a hill,
She put a mouse in a bag,
   And sent it to mill;

The miller declared,
   By the point of his knife,
He never took toll
   Of a mouse in his life.

The following is part of a comic song called "Success to the Whistle and Wig," intended to be sung in rotation by the members of a club.

THERE was an old woman had three sons,
Jerry, and James, and John;
Jerry was hung, James was drowned,
John was lost and never was found,
And there was an end of the three sons,
Jerry, and James, and John!

———

OLD Betty Blue
Lost a holiday shoe,
What can old Betty do?
Give her another
To match the other,
And then she may swagger
in two.

The tale on which the following story is founded is found in a MS. of
the fifteenth century, preserved in the Chetham Library at Manchester.

THERE was an old man who lived in a wood,
    As you may plainly see;
He said he could do as much work in a day,
    As his wife could do in three.
"With all my heart," the old woman said;
    "If that you will allow,
To-morrow you'll stay at home in my stead,
    And I'll go drive the plough;
But you must milk the Tidy cow,
    For fear that she go dry;
And you must feed the little pigs
    That are within the stye;
And you must mind the speckled hen,
    For fear she lay away;
And you must reel the spool of yarn
    That I span yesterday."

The old woman took a staff in her hand,
    And went to drive the plough;
The old man took a pail in his hand,
    And went to milk the cow;

But Tidy hinched, and Tidy flinched,
    And Tidy broke his nose,
And Tidy gave him such a blow,
    That the blood ran down to his toes.

"High! Tidy! ho! Tidy! high!
    Tidy, do stand still!
If ever I milk you, Tidy, again,
    'Twill be sore against my will."
He went to feed the little pigs,
    That were within the stye;
He hit his head against the beam
    And he made the blood to fly.

He went to mind the speckled hen,
    For fear she'd lay astray,
And he forgot the spool of yarn
    His wife spun yesterday.

So he swore by the sun, the moon, and the stars,
    And the green leaves on the tree,
If his wife didn't do a day's work in her life,
    She should ne'er be ruled by he.

    THERE was an old woman,
        And she sold puddings and pies:
    She went to the mill,
        And the dust flew in her eyes:
    "Hot pies and cold pies to sell!"
        Wherever she goes—
    You may follow her by the smell.

Oh, dear, what can the matter be?
Two old women got up in an apple-tree;
    One came down,
And the other stayed till Saturday.

DAME Trot and her cat
　　Led a peaceable life
When they were not troubled
　　With other folks' strife.

When Dame had her dinner
　　Near Pussy would wait,
And was sure to receive
　　A nice piece from her plate.

THERE was an old man,   He took him out of the stall,
And he had a calf,   And put him on the wall;
  And that's half;   And that's all.

FATHER Short came down the lane,
  Oh! I'm obliged to hammer and smite
  From four in the morning till eight at night,
For a bad master and a worse dame.

    THERE was an old woman
      Lived under a hill;
    And if she's not gone,
      She lives there still.

There was an old woman of Norwich,
Who lived upon nothing but porridge;
 Parading the town,
 She turned cloak into gown,
This thrifty old woman of Norwich.

There was an old woman in Surrey,
Who was morn, noon, and night in a hurry,
 Called her husband a fool,
 Drove the children to school,
The worrying old woman of Surrey.

There was an old woman called Nothing-at-all,
Who rejoiced in a dwelling exceedingly small;
A man stretched his mouth to its utmost extent,
And down at one gulp house and old woman went.

A LITTLE old man and I fell out:
How shall we bring this matter about?
Bring it about as well as you can—
Get you gone, you little old man!

OLD Mother Niddity
Nod swore by the
pudding-bag,
She would go to Sto-
ken Church Fair;
And then old Father
Peter said he would
meet her
Before she got half-
way there.

THERE was an old woman tossed up in a basket,
　Nineteen times as high as the moon;
Where she was going I couldn't but ask it,
　For in her hand she carried a broom.

Old woman, old woman, old woman, quoth I,
O whither, O whither, O whither so high?
To brush the cobwebs off the sky!
Shall I go with thee? Aye, by-and-bye.

THERE was an old man who lived in Middle Row,
He had five hens and a name for them, oh!
Bill and Ned and Battock,
Cut-her-foot and Pattock,
Chuck, my Lady Prattock,
Go to thy nest and lay.

THERE was an old woman of Leeds
Who spent all her time in good deeds;
She worked for the poor
Till her fingers were sore,
This pious old woman of Leeds!

TENTH CLASS.

Games.

Come, my children, come away,
For the sun shines bright to-day;
Little children, come with me,
Birds and brooks and posies see;
Get your hats and come away,
For it is a pleasant day.

Everything is laughing, singing,
All the pretty flowers are springing;
See the kitten, full of fun,
Sporting in the brilliant sun;
Children too may sport and play,
For it is a pleasant day.

[178]

Bring the hoop, and bring the ball,
Come with happy faces all;
Let us make a merry ring,
Talk and laugh, and dance and sing.
Quickly, quickly, come away,
For it is a pleasant day.

Rhymes used by children to decide who is to begin a game.

ONE-ERY, two-ery,
   Ziccary zan;
Hollow bone, crack a bone,
   Ninery, ten:
Spittery spot,
   It must be done;
Twiddleum twaddleum,
   Twenty-one.

Hink spink, the puddings stink,
  The fat begins to fry,
Nobody at home, but jumping Joan,
  Father, mother, and I.
Stick, stock, stone dead,
  Blind man can't see,
Every knave will have a slave,
  You or I must be he.

DANCE, Thumbkin, dance,
      [Keep the thumb in motion.
Dance, ye merrymen, every one;
      [All the fingers in motion.
For Thumbkin, he can dance alone,
      [The thumb only moving.
Thumbkin, he can dance alone,
      [Ditto.
Dance, Foreman, dance,
      [The first finger moving.
Dance, ye merrymen, every one;
      [The whole moving.
But Foreman, he can dance alone,
Foreman, he can dance alone.

And so on with the others—naming the second finger
"Longman," the third finger "Ringman," and the
fourth finger "Littleman." Littleman cannot dance
alone.

The following is used by schoolboys when two are starting to run a race.

ONE to make ready,
  And two to prepare;
Good luck to the rider,
  And away goes the mare.

THE FOX.

In a children's game, where all the little actors are seated in a circle, the following stanza is used as question and answer:

Who goes round my house this night?
None but cruel Tom!
Who steals all the sheep at night?
None but this poor one.

One child holds a wand or pen or stick to the face of another, repeating these lines, and making grimaces, to cause the latter to laugh, and so to the others: those who laugh paying a forfeit.

Buff says Buff to all his men,
And I say Buff to you again;
Buff neither laughs nor smiles,
But carries his face with a very good grace,
And passes the stick to the very next place!

Queen Anne, Queen Anne, you sit in the sun,
As fair as a lily, as white as a wand.
I send you three letters, and pray read one:
You must read one, if you can't read all;
So pray, Miss or Master, throw up the ball!

Highty Lock O!
To London we go,
To York we ride;
And Edward has pussy-cat tied to his side;
He shall have little dog tied to the other,
And then he goes trid-trod to see his grandmother.

Gay go up and gay go down,
To ring the bells of London town.

Bulls' eyes and targets,
Say the bells of St. Marg'ret's.

Brickbats and tiles,
Say the bells of St. Giles'.

Halfpence and farthings,
Say the bells of St. Mar-
tin's.

Oranges and lemons,
Say the bells of St. Clem-
ent's.

Pancakes and fritters,
Say the bells of St. Peters.

Two sticks and an apple,
Say the bells at White-
chapel.

Old Father Baldpate,
Say the slow bells at Ald-
gate.

You owe me ten shillings,
Say the bells at St. Hel-
en's.

Pokers and tongs,
Say the bells at St. John's.

Kettles and pans,
Say the bells of St. Ann's.

When will you pay me?
Say the bells of Old Bailey.

When I grow rich,
Say the bells at Shore-
ditch.

Pray when will that be?
Say the bells of Stepney.

I am sure I don't know,
Says the great bell at Bow.

Here comes a candle to light you to bed,
And here comes a chopper to chop off your head.

At the conclusion the captive is privately asked if he will have oranges or lemons (the two leaders of the arch having previously agreed which designation shall belong to each), and he goes behind the one he may chance to name. When all are thus divided into two parties, they conclude the game by trying to pull each other beyond a certain line.

HEWLEY-PULEY.

THE children are seated and the following questions put by one of the party, holding a twisted handkerchief or something of the sort in the hand. The handkerchief is called "hewley-puley," and the questions are asked by the child who holds it. If one answers wrongly, a box on the ear with the handkerchief is the consequence; but if they all reply correctly, then the one who breaks silence first has that punishment.

Take this. What's this ?—Hewley-puley.
Where's my share ?—About the kite's neck.
Where's the kite ?—Flown to the wood.
Where's the wood ?—The fire has burned it.
Where's the fire ?—The water has quenched it.
Where's the water ?—The ox has drunk it.
Where's the ox ?—The butcher has killed it.
Where's the butcher ?—The rope has hanged him.
Where's the rope ?—The rat has gnawed it.
Where's the rat ?—The cat has killed it.
Where's the cat ?—Behind the church-door, cracking pebble-stones and marrow-bones for yours and my supper, and the one who speaks first shall have a box on the ear.

AWAKE, arise, pull out your eyes,
And hear what time of day;
And when you have done, pull out your tongue,
And see what you can say.

HERE goes my lord
A trot, a trot, a trot, a trot!
Here goes my lady
A canter, a canter, a canter, a canter!

Here goes my young master
Jockey-hitch, Jockey-hitch, Jockey-hitch, Jockey-hitch!
Here goes my young miss
An amble, an amble, an amble, an amble!
The footman lags behind to tipple ale and wine,
And goes gallop, a gallop, a gallop, to make up his time.

Ride a cock-horse to Banbury Cross,
To buy little Johnny a galloping horse;
It trots behind, and it ambles before,
And Johnny shall ride till he can ride no more.

Sieve my lady's oatmeal,
    Grind my lady's flour,
Put it in a chestnut,
    Let it stand an hour;
One may rush, two may rush,—
Come, my girls, walk under the bush.

Trip and go, heave and hoe!
Up and down, to and fro;
From the town to the grove,
Two and two let us rove,
A-maying, a-playing;
Love hath no gainsaying!
So, merrily trip and go!
So, merrily trip and go!

See-saw, jack a daw!
What is a craw to do wi' her?
She has not a stocking to put on her,
And the craw has not one for to gi' her.

Now we dance looby, looby, looby,
Now we dance looby, looby, light
Shake your right hand a little,
And turn you round about.

Now we dance looby, looby, looby,
Shake your right hand a little,
Shake your left hand a little,
And turn you round about.

Now we dance looby, looby, looby,
Shake your right hand a little,
Shake your left hand a little,
Shake your right foot a little,
And turn you round about.

Now we dance looby, looby, looby,
Shake your right hand a little,
Shake your left hand a little,
Shake your right foot a little,
Shake your left foot a little,
And turn you round about.

Now we dance looby, looby, looby,
Shake your right hand a little,
Shake your left hand a little,
Shake your right foot a little,
Shake your left foot a little,
Shake your head a little,
And turn you round about.

Children dance round first, then stop and shake the hand, &c., then turn slowly round, and then dance in a ring again.

MARGERY MUTTON-PIE and Johnny Bopeep.
They met together in Gracechurch Street;
In and out, in and out, over the way,
"Oh, says Johnny, "'t is chop-nose day!"

THE BRAMBLE-BUSH.

A ring-dance imitation play, the metrical portion of which is not
without a little melody. The bramble-bush is often imaginative, but
sometimes represented by a child in the centre of the ring; all join
hands, and dance round in a circle, singing,

Here we go round the bramble-bush,
The bramble-bush, the bramble-bush;
Here we go round the bramble-bush
On a cold frosty morning!

After the chanting of this verse is ended, all the children commence an imitation of washing clothes, making appropriate movements with their hands, and saying,

This is the way we wash our clothes,
Wash our clothes, wash our clothes;
This is the way we wash our clothes
On a cold frosty morning!

They then dance round, repeating the first stanza, after which the operation of drying the clothes is commenced with a similar verse, "This is the way we dry our clothes," &c. The game may be continued almost *ad infinitum* by increasing the number of duties to be performed. They are, however, generally satisfied with mangling, *smoothing*, or ironing the clothes, and then putting them away. Sometimes they conclude with a general cleaning, which may well be necessary after the large quantity of work which has been done:

This is the way we clean our rooms,
Clean our rooms, clean our rooms;
This is the way we clean our rooms
On a cold frosty morning!

And, like good merry washing-women, they are not exhausted with their labors, but conclude with the song, "Here we go round the bramble-bush," having had sufficient exercise to warm themselves on any "cold frosty morning," which was doubtless the result, we may observe *en passant*, as a matter of domestic economy aimed at by the author. It is not so easy to give a similar explanation to the game of the mulberry-bush, conducted in the same manner:

Here we go round the mulberry-bush,
The mulberry-bush, the mulberry-bush;
Here we go round the mulberry-bush
On a sunshiny morning.

In this game the motion-cries are usually "This is the way we wash our clothes," "This is the way we dry our clothes," "This is the way we make our shoes," "This is the way we mend our shoes," "This is the way the gentlemen walk," "This is the way the ladies walk," &c., As in other cases, the dance may be continued by the addition of cries and motions, which may be rendered pretty and characteristic in the hands of judicious actors. This game, however, requires too much exercise to render it so appropriate to the season as the other.

DROP-GLOVE.

CHILDREN stand round in a circle, leaving a space between each. One walks round the outside, and carries a glove or handkerchief in her hand, saying,

> I've a glove in my hand,
> > Hittity Hot!
> Another in my other hand,
> > Hotter than that!
> So I sow beans, and so they come up,
> Some in a mug, and some in a cup.
> I sent a letter to my love,
> I lost it, I lost it!
> I found it, I found it!
> It burns, it scalds.

Repeating the last words very rapidly till she drops the glove behind one of them, and whoever has the glove must overtake her, following her exactly in and out till she catches her. If the pursuer makes a mistake in the pursuit, she loses, and the game is over; otherwise she continues the game with the glove.

> INTERY, mintery, cutery-corn,
> Apple seed and apple thorn;
> Wine, brier, limber-lock,
> Five geese in a flock,
> Sit and sing by a spring,
> O-u-t, and in again.

> TIP top, tower
> Tumble down in an hour.

First pig went to market,
Second pig stayed at home,
Third pig had roast beef
And fourth pig had none;
Fifth little pig said, "wee, wee,
Give me some!"

THE OLD DAME.

ONE child, called the Old Dame, sits on the floor, and the rest joining hands, form a circle round her, and dancing, sing the following lines:

Children.   To Beccles! to Beccles!
              To buy a bunch of nettles!
              Pray, old Dame, what's o'clock?
Dame.   One, going for two.
Children.   To Beccles! to Beccles!
              To buy a bunch of nettles!
              Pray, old Dame, what's o'clock?
Dame.   Two, going for three.

And so on till she reaches "Eleven, going for twelve." After this the following questions are asked with the replies.—*C.* Where have you been? *D.* To the wood.

C. What for? *D.* To pick up sticks. *C.* What for?
D. To light my fire. *C.* What for? *D.* To boil my
kettle. *C.* What for? *D.* To cook some of your
chickens. The children then all run away as fast as
they can, and the Old Dame tries to catch one of them.
Whoever is caught is the next to personate the Dame.

In the game where the following lines are used, one person goes round
inside a ring of children, clapping a cap between his hands. When he
drops it at the foot of any one, that one leaves his position and gives
chase, and is obliged to thread the very same course among the children
till the first is caught. The first then stands with his back towards the
centre of the ring, the one called out takes his place, and thus they con-
tinue till nearly all are "turned."

My hand burns hot, hot, hot,
And whoever I love best, I'll drop this at his foot!

NIDDY-NODDY.

A SIMPLE but very amusing game at cards, at which any number can
play. The cards are dealt round, and one person commences the game
by placing down a card, and the persons next in succession who hold the
same card in the various suits place them down upon it, the holder of the
last winning the trick. The four persons who hold the cards say, when
they put them down,

1. There's a good card for thee.
2. There's a still better than he.
3. There's the best of all three.
4. And there is Niddy-noddee!

The person who is first *out*, receives a fish for each card unplayed.

A GAME AT BALL.

Cuckoo, cherry-tree,
Catch a bird, and give it to
me;

Let the tree be high or low,
Let it hail, rain, or snow.

BARLEY-BRIDGE.

A STRING of boys and girls, each holding by his predecessor's skirts, approaches two others, who, with joined and elevated hands, form a double arch. After the dialogue is concluded, the line passes through the arch, and the last is caught, if possible, by the sudden lowering of the arms.

"How many miles to Barley bridge?"
"Threescore and ten."
"Can I get there by candlelight?"
"Yes, if your legs be long."
"A courtesy to you, and a courtesy to you,
If you please will you let the King's horses through?"
"Through and through shall they go,
 For the King's sake;
 But the one that is hindmost
 Will meet with a great mistake."

THE game of water-skimming is of high antiquity, being mentioned by Julius Pollux, and also by Eustathius, in his commentary upon Homer. Brand quotes a curious passage from Minucius Felix; but all antiquaries seem to have overlooked the very curious notice in Higgins' adaptation of Junius's "Nomenclator," 8vo, London, 1585, p. 299, where it is called "a duck and a drake, and a halfe-penie cake." Thus it is probable that lines like the following were employed in this game as early as 1585; and it may be that the last line has recently furnished a hint to Mathews in his amusing song in "Patter *v.* Clatter."

A DUCK and a drake,
A nice barley-cake,
With a penny to pay the
old baker;

A hop and a scotch,
Is another notch,
Slitherum, slatherum, take
her.

Two children sit opposite to each other; the first turns her fingers one over the other, and says,

"May my geese fly over your barn?"

The other answers "Yes, if they'll do no harm," upon which the first unpacks the fingers of her hand, and, waving it overhead, says,

"Fly over his barn, and eat all his corn."

SEE-SAW.

A COMMON game, children vacillating on either end of a plank supported on its centre. While enjoying this recreation, they have a song of appropriate cadence, the burden of which is,

Titty cum tawtay,   Titty cum tawtay,
   The ducks in the water: The geese follow after.

To market ride the gentlemen,
   So do we, so do we;
Then comes the country clown,
   Hobbledy gee, Hobbledy gee;
First go the ladies, nim, nim, nim;
Next come the gentlemen, trim, trim, trim;
Then come the country clowns, gallop-a-trot.

Nettles grow in an angry bush,
An angry bush, an angry bush;
Nettles grow in an angry bush,
With my High, Ho, Ham!
This is the way the lady goes,
The lady goes, the lady goes;
This is the way the lady goes,
With my High, Ho, Ham!

The children dance round some chairs, singing the first three lines, turning round and clapping hands for the fourth line. They curtsey while saying "this is the way the lady goes," and again turn round and clap hands for the last line. The same process is followed in every verse, only varying what they act: thus, in the third verse, they *bow* for the gentleman.

Nettles grow in an angry bush, &c.,
This is the way the gentleman goes, &c.
Nettles grow in an angry bush, &c.
This is the way the tailor goes, &c.

And so the amusement is protracted *ad libitum* with shoemaking, washing the clothes, ironing, churning, milking, making up butter, &c.

There were two
blackbirds
Sitting on a hill,
The one named Jack,
The other named
· Jill;

Fly away, Jack!   Come again, Jack!
Fly away, Jill!   Come again, Jill!

Ride a cock-horse to Banbury Cross,
To see what Tommy can buy;
A penny white loaf, a penny white cake,
And a twopenny apple pie.

SEE-SAW, Margery Daw,
Sold her bed and lay upon straw;
Was not she a dirty girl
To sell her bed and lie in dirt?

Game with the hands.

PEASE-PUDDING hot,
  Pease pudding cold,
Pease-pudding in the pot,
  Nine days old.

Some like it hot,
  Some like it cold,
Some like it in the pot,
  Nine days old.

MARY BROWN. FAIR GUNDELA.

A slightly dramatic character may be observed in this game, which was obtained from Essex, England. Children form a ring, one girl kneeling in the centre, and sorrowfully hiding her face with her hands. One in the ring then says:

> Here we all stand round the ring,
> And now we shut poor Mary in;
> Rise up, poor Mary Brown,
> And see your poor mother go through the town.

To this she answers:

> I will not stand up upon my feet,
> To see my poor mother go through the street.

The children then cry:

> Rise up, rise up, poor Mary Brown,
> And see your poor father go through the town.

Mary. I will not stand up upon my feet,
> To see my poor father go through the street.

Children. Rise up, rise up, poor Mary Brown,
> To see your poor brother go through the town.

Mary. I will not stand up upon my feet,
> To see my poor brother go through the street.

Children. Rise up, rise up, poor Mary Brown,
> To see your poor sister go through the town.

Mary. I will not stand up upon my feet,
> To see my poor sister go through the street.

Children. Rise up, rise up, poor Mary Brown,
> To see the poor beggars go through the town.

Mary. I will not stand up upon my feet,
> To see the poor beggars go through the street.

One would have thought that this tiresome repetition had been continued quite long enough; but two other verses are sometimes added, introducing *gentlemen* and *ladies* with the same questions, to both of which it is unnecessary to say that the callous and hard-hearted Mary Brown replies with perfect indifference and want of curiosity. All versions, however, conclude with the girls saying:

> Rise up, rise up, poor Mary Brown,
> And see your poor sweetheart go through the town.

The chord is at last touched, and Mary, frantically replying,

> I will get up upon my feet,
> To see my sweetheart go through the street!

rushes with impetuosity to break the ring, and generally succeeds in escaping the bonds that detain her from her imaginary love.

Leader.	I went up one pair of stairs.
1st Child.	Just like me.
Leader.	I went up two pair of stairs.
2nd Child.	Just like me.
Leader.	I went into a room.
3rd Child.	Just like me.
Leader.	I looked out of a window.
4th Child.	Just like me.
Leader.	And there I saw a monkey.
5th Child.	Just like me!

Leader.	I am a gold lock.
1st Child.	I am a gold key.
Leader.	I am a silver lock.
2nd Child.	I am a silver key.
Leader.	I am a brass lock.
3rd Child.	I am a brass key.
Leader.	I am a lead lock.
4th Child.	I am a lead key.
Leader.	I am a monk lock.
5th Child.	I am a monk key!

The following lines are sung by children when starting for a race.

> GOOD horses, bad horses,   Three o'clock, four o'clock,
> What is the time of day?   Now fare you away.

THERE was a man, and his name was Dob,
And he had a wife, and her name was Mob,
And he had a dog, and he called it Cob,
And she had a cat, called Chitterabob.
    Cob, says Dob,
    Chitterabob, says Mob,
    Cob was Dob's dog,
    Chitterabob Mob's cat.

Two of the strongest children are selected, *A* and *B ; A* stands within a ring of the children, *B* being outside.

A. Who is going round my sheepfold?
B. Only poor old Jacky Lingo.
A. Don't steal any of my black sheep.
B. No, no more I will, only by one:
    Up! says Jacky Lingo.   (*Strikes one.*)

The child struck leaves the ring, and takes hold of *B* behind; *B* in the same manner takes the other children, one by one, gradually increasing his tail on each repetition of the verses, until he has got the whole; *A* then tries to get them back; *B* runs away with them; they try to shelter themselves behind *B; A* drags them off, one by one, setting them against a wall until he has recovered all.—A regular "tearing game," as children say.

RIDE a cock-horse to Banbury Cross,
To see an old lady upon a white horse,
Rings on her fingers, and bells on her toes,
And so she makes music wherever she goes.

ONE old Oxford ox opening oysters;
Two teetotums totally tired of trying to trot to Tadbury;
Three tall tigers tippling tenpenny tea;
Four fat friars fanning fainting flies;
Five frippy Frenchmen foolishly fishing for flies;
Six sportsmen shooting snipes;
Seven Severn salmons swallowing shrimps;
Eight Englishmen eagerly examining Europe;
Nine nimble noblemen nibbling nonpareils;
Ten tinkers tinkling upon ten tin tinder-boxes with ten
　　tenpenny tacks;
Eleven elephants elegantly equipt;
Twelve typographical typographers typically translating
　　types.

Ride a cock-horse to Coventry Cross,
  To see what Emma can buy;
A penny white cake I'll buy for her sake,
  And a twopenny tart or a pie.

THE TOWN LOVERS.

A GAME played by boys and girls. A girl is placed in the middle of a ring, and says the following lines, the names being altered to suit the party. She points to each one named, and at the last line the party selected immediately runs away, and if the girl catches him, he pays a forfeit, or the game is commenced again, the boy being placed in the middle, and the lines, *mutatis mutandis*, serve for a reversed amusement:

There is a girl of our town,
She often wears a flowered gown:
Tommy loves her night and day,
And Richard when he may,
And Johnny when he can:
I think Sam will be the man!

———

THIS is the way the ladies ride;
　Tri, tre, tre, tree,
　Tri, tre, tre, tree!
This is the way the ladies ride,
　Tri, tre, tre, tre, tri-tre-tre-tree!

This is the way the gentlemen ride;
　Gallop-a-trot,
　Gallop-a-trot!
This is the way the gentlemen ride,
　Gallop-a-gallop-a-trot!

This is the way the farmers ride,
　Hobbledy-hoy,
　Hobbledy-hoy!
This is the way the farmers ride,
　Hobbledy hobbledy-hoy!

———

TOM Brown's two little Indian boys,
　One ran away,
　The other wouldn't stay,—
Tom Brown's two little Indian boys.

A Christmas custom in Lancashire. The boys dress themselves up with ribbons, and perform various pantomimes, after which one of them, who has a blackened face, a rough skin coat, and a broom in his hand, sings as follows:

HERE come I,
  Little David Doubt;
If you don't give me money,
  I'll sweep you all out.

Money I want,
  And money I crave;
You don't give me money,
  I'll sweep you all to the
        grave!

THIS is the key of the kingdom.
In that kingdom there is a city.
In that city there is a town.
In that town there is a street.
In that street there is a lane.
In that lane there is a yard.
In that yard there is a house.
In that house there is a room.
In that room there is a bed.
On that bed there is a basket.
In that basket there are some flowers.
Flowers in the basket, basket in the bed, bed in the
    room, &c., &c.

THIS should be accompanied by a kind of pantomimic dance, in which the motions of the body and arms express the process of weaving; the motion of the shuttle, &c.

Weave the diaper tick-a-tick tick,
Weave the diaper tick—
Come this way, come that,
As close as a mat,
Athwart and across, up and down, round about,
And forwards, and backwards, and inside, and out;
Weave the diaper thick-a-thick thick,
Weave the diaper thick!

THIS game begins thus: "Take this." "What's this?" "A gaping, wide-mouthed, waddling frog," &c.

Twelve huntsmen with horns and hounds,
Hunting over other men's grounds;
Eleven ships sailing o'er the main,
Some bound for France and some for Spain:
I wish them all safe home again;
Ten comets in the sky,
Some low and some high;
Nine peacocks in the air,
I wonder how they all came there,
I do not know and I do not care;
Eight joiners in Joiners' Hall,
Working with the tools and all;
Seven lobsters in a dish,
As fresh as any heart could wish;
Six beetles against the wall,
Close by an old woman's apple-stall;
Five puppies of our dog Ball,
Who daily for their breakfast call;
Four horses stuck in a bog,
Three monkeys tied to a clog;
Two pudding-ends would choke a dog,
With a gaping, wide-mouthed, waddling frog.

CLAP hands, clap hands,
    Hie Tommy Randy,
Did you see my good man?
    They call him Cock-a-bandy.

Silken stockings on his legs,
    Silver buckles glancin,'
A sky-blue bonnet on his head,
    And oh! but he is handsome.

Number number nine,
   this hoop's mine;
Number number ten,
   take it back again.

This is acted by two or more girls, who walk or dance up and down, turning when they say "Turn, cheeses, turn." The "green cheeses," as we are informed, are made with sage and potato-tops. Two girls are said to be "cheese and cheese."

Green cheese, yellow
   laces,
Up and down the mar-
   ket-places,
   Turn, cheeses, turn.

A NUMBER of boys and girls stand round one in the middle, who repeats the following lines, counting the children until one is counted out by the end of the verses.

Ring me (1), ring me (2), ring me rary (3),
As I go round (4), ring by ring (5),
A virgin (6) goes a-maying (7).
Here's a flower (8), and there's a flower (9),
Growing in my lady's garden (10),
If you set your foot awry (11),
Gentle John will make you cry (12),
If you set your foot amiss (13),
Gentle John (14) will give you a kiss.

The child upon whom (14) falls is then taken out, and forced to select one of the other sex. The middle child then proceeds.

This [lady or gentleman] is none of ours,
Has put [him or her] self in [the selected child's] power,
So clap all hands, and ring all bells, and make the wed-
   ding o'er. *(All clap hands.)*

If the child taken by lot joins in the clapping, the selected child is rejected, and I believe takes the middle place. Otherwise, I think there is a salute.

THE "Three Knights of Spain" is a game played in the following manner: The *dramatis personæ* form themselves in two parties—one representing a courtly dame and her daughters, the other the suitors of the daughters. The last party, moving backwards and forwards, with their arms entwined, approach and recede from the mother party, which is stationary, singing to a very sweet air.

Suitors. We are three brethren out of Spain,
       Come to court your daughter Jane.

Mother. My daughter Jane she is too young,
       And has not learned her mother tongue.

Suitors. Be she young, or be she old,
       For her beauty she must be sold.
       So fare you well, my lady gay,
       We'll call again another day.

Mother. Turn back, turn back, thou scornful knight,
       And rub thy spurs till they be bright.

Suitors. Of my spurs take thou no thought,
       For in this town they were not bought;
       So fare you well, my lady gay,
       We'll call again another day.

Mother. Turn back, turn back, thou scornful knight,
       And take the fairest in your sight.

Suitor. The fairest maid that I can see
       Is pretty Nancy,—come to me.*

 * Here the suitor tries to pull Nancy over to his side.

       Here comes your daughter safe and sound,
       Every pocket with a thousand pound·
       Every finger with a gay gold ring;
       Please to take your daughter in.

BEANS AND BUTTER.

So the game of "Hide-and-Seek" is called in some parts of Oxfordshire.

CHILDREN hide from each other, and when it is time to commence the search, the cry is,

   -   Hot boiled beans and very good butter,
       If you please to come to supper!

HERE we come a-piping,
First in Spring, and then in May;
The Queen she sits upon the sand,
Fair as a lily, white as a wand:
King John has sent you letters three,—
And begs you'll read them unto me.
We can't read one without them all,
So pray, Miss Bridget, deliver the ball!

HITTY-TITTY.

HITTY-TITTY indoors
Hitty-titty out;

You touch Hitty-titty,
And Hitty-titty will bite
you.

These lines are said by children when one of them has hid herself. They then run away, and the one who is bitten (caught) becomes Hitty-titty, and hides in her turn.

ANOTHER game, played exclusively by boys. Two, who are fixed upon for the purpose, leave the group, and privately arrange that the pass-word shall be some implement of a particular trade. The trade is announced in the dialogue, and then the fun is, that the unfortunate wight who guesses the "tool" is beaten with the caps of his fellows till he reaches a fixed goal, after which he goes out in turn.

"Two broken tradesmen,
  Newly come over,
The one from France and Scotland,
  The other from Dover."
"What's your trade?"

Carpenters, nailers, smiths, tinkers, or any other is answered, and on guessing the instrument "plane him!" "hammer him!" "rasp him!" or "solder him!" is called out respectively during the period of punishment.

Used in Somersetshire in counting out the game of pee-wip or pee-wit.

ONE-ERY, two-ery, hickary, hum,
Fillison, follison, Nicholson, John,
Quever, quauver, Irish Mary,
Stenkarum, stankarum, buck!

" his little pig went
to market.

This little pig stayed
at home.

This little pig
got roast beef.

This little pig got none.

This little pig cried Oh! dear me, all the way home.

WHOOP, whoop, and hollow,
Good dogs won't follow,
Without the hare cries "pee
wit."

THE following is a game played as follows: A string of boys and girls,
each holding by the predecessor's skirts, approach two others, who with
joined and elevated hands form a double arch.   After the dialogue, the
line passes through, and the last is caught by a sudden lowering of the
arms—if possible.

How many miles is it to Babylon?—
Threescore miles and ten.
Can I get there by candlelight?—
Yes, and back again!
If your heels are nimble and light,
You may get there by candlelight.

CLAP hands, clap hands!
Till father comes home;
For father's got money,
But mother's got none.
Clap hands, &c.
Till father, &c.

GAME OF THE GIPSY.

ONE child is selected for Gipsy, one for Mother, and one for Daughter
Sue. The Mother says,

I charge my daughters every one
To keep good house while I am gone.
You and *you (points)* but specially *you,*
[*Or sometimes,* "but specially *Sue* "]
Or else I'll beat you black and blue.

During the Mother's absence the Gipsy comes in, entices a child away,
and hides her.   This process is repeated till all the children are hidden,
when the Mother has to find them.

HERE stands a post,
Who put it there?
A better man than you;
Touch it if you dare!

A STRING of children, hand in hand, stand in a row. A child (*A*) stands in front of them, as leader; two other children (*B* and *C*; form an arch, each holding both the hands of the other.

A. Draw a pail of water,
   For my lady's daughter;
   My father's a King, and my mother's a Queen,
   My two little sisters are dressed in green,
   Stamping grass and parsley,
   Marigold-leaves and daisies.

B. One rush, two rush,
   Pray thee, fine lady, come under my bush.

A passes by under the arch, followed by the whole string of children, the last of whom is taken captive by *B* and *C*. The verses are repeated until all are taken.

A STANDS with a row of girls (her daughters) behind her; *B*, a suitor, advances.

B. Trip trap over the grass. If you please will you let
   .one of your [eldest] daughters come,
   Come and dance with me ?
   I will give you pots and pans, I will give you brass,
   I will give you anything for a pretty lass.

A says, "No."

B. I will give you gold and silver, I will give you pearl,
   I will give you anything for a pretty girl.

A. Take one, take one, the fairest you may see.

B. The fairest one that I can see
   Is pretty Nancy,—come to me.

B carries one off, and says,

   You shall have a duck, my dear, and you shall have
      a drake,
   And you shall have a young man apprentice for
      your sake.

Children say,

   If this young man should happen to die,
      And leave this poor woman a widow,
   The bells shall all ring, and the birds shall all sing,
      And we'll all clap hands together.

So it is repeated until the whole are taken.

Children hunting bats.

BAT, bat (*clap hands*),
Come under my hat,
And I'll give you a slice of
   bacon;

And when I bake,
I'll give you a cake,
If I am not mistaken.

SEE-SAW sacradown,
Which is the way to London town?
One foot up and the other down,
And that is the way to London town.

GAMES ON A CHILD'S FEATURES.

HERE sits the Lord Mayor . . . *forehead.*
  Here sit his two men . . . *eyes.*
Here sits the cock . . . . . *right cheek.*
  Here sits the hen . . . . *left cheek.*
Here sit the little chickens . . *tip of nose.*
  Here the run in . . . . . *mouth.*
Chinchopper, chinchopper,
  Chinchopper, chin! . . . . *chuck the chin.*

THESE lines are said to a very young child, touching successively for each line the eye, nose, chin, tooth, tongue, and mouth.

Bo peeper,	White lopper,
Nose dreeper,	Red rag,
Chin chopper,	And little gap.

Sometimes the following version is used.

Brow brinky,	Nose noppy,
Eye winky,	Cheek cherry,
Chin choppy,	Mouth merry.

A PLAY WITH THE FACE.

The child exclaims:

Ring the bell! . . *giving a lock of its hair a pull.*
Knock at the door . *tapping its forehead.*
Draw the latch! . . *pulling up its nose.*
And walk in . . *opening its mouth and putting in its finger.*

In the following, the various parts of the countenance are touched as the lines are repeated, and at the close the chin is struck playfully, that the tongue may be gently bitten.

Eye winker,	Mouth eater,
Tom Tinker,	Chin chopper,
Nose dropper,	Chin chopper.

THUMB bold,	Lick-apan,
Thibity-thold,	Mamma's little man.
Langman,	

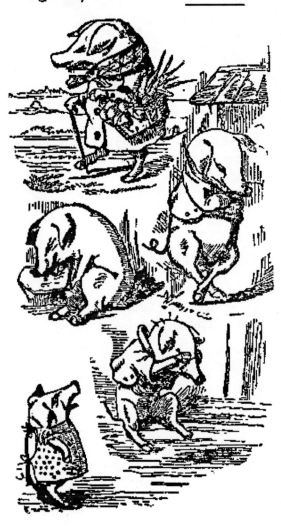

THIS broke the barn,
This stole the corn,
This got none,
This went pinky-winky
All the way home!

1. THIS pig went to the barn.
2. This eat all the corn.
3. This said he would tell.
4. This said he wasn't well.
5. This went Week! week! week! over the door sill.

A song set to five fingers.

1. THIS pig went to market;
2. This pig stayed at home;
3. This pig had a bit of meat;
4. And this pig had none;
5. This pig said, Wee, wee, wee!
   I can't find my way home.

A game on the slate.

EGGS, butter, bread,
Stick, stock, stone dead!
Stick him up, stick him down,
Stick him in the old man's crown.

From Yorkshire.   A game to alarm children.

FLOWERS, flowers, high-
   do!
Sheeny, greeny, rino!

Sheeny, greeny,
Sheeny, greeny,
   Rum tum fra!

SEE-SAW, Margary Daw,
   Little Jacky shall have a new master;
   Little Jacky shall have but a penny a day,
   Because he can't work any faster.

A GAME OF THE FOX.

Fox a fox, a brummalary,
   How many miles to Lummafiary? Lummabary?
A. Eight and eight and a hundred and eight.
   How shall I get home to-night?
A. Spin your legs, and run fast.

In the following childish amusement, one extends his arm, and the other, in illustration of the narrative, strikes him gently with the side of his hand at the shoulder and wrist, and then at the word "middle" with considerable force on the flexor muscles at the elbow-joint.

My father was a French-
   man,
   He bought for me a
     fiddle,
He cut me here he cut
   me there,
   He cut me right in
     the middle.

I went to the sea,
And saw twentee
   Geese all in a row:
My glove I would give
Full of gold, if my wife
   Was as white as those.

These lines are to be re-
peated rapidly and correctly,
inserting the word *cother* after
every word, under pain of a
forfeit.

It's time, I believe,
For us to get leave;
The little dog says
It isn't, it is; it isn't it is do.

Said by a schoolboy, who places his book between his knees. His two forefingers are then placed together, and the breadth of each is measured alternately along the length of the book. The time to get leave (to be dismissed) is supposed to have arrived or not according as one finger or the other fills up the last place.

A duck and a drake, It's time to go home,
And a white penny cake. It isn't, it is, &c.

So going on with the fingers one over the other along the edge of a book or desk, till the last finger determines the question.

———

PUT your finger in Foxy's Foxy is at the back door,
 hole, Picking of a bone.
Foxy is not at home:

Holding the fist in such a way that if a child puts its finger in you can secure it, still leaving the hole at top open.

———

THIS pig went to market,
 Squeak mouse, mouse, mousey;
Shoe, shoe, shoe the wild colt,
 And here's my own doll, Dowsy.

Song set to five toes.

1. LET us go to the wood, said this pig;
2. What to do there? says that pig;
3. To look for my mother, says this pig;
4. What to do with her? says that pig;
5. Kiss her to death, says this pig.

Jᴀᴄᴋ's alive, and in very good health;
If he dies in your hand, you must look to yourself.

Played with a stick, one end burnt red hot; it is passed round a circle from one to the other, the one who passes it saying this, and the one whose hand it goes out in paying a forfeit.

_____

Patting the foot on the five toes.

Sʜᴏᴇ the colt, shoe!
  Shoe the wild mare;
Put a sack on her back,
  See if she'll bear.
If she'll bear.
We'll give her some grains;
  If she won't bear,
We'll dash out her brains!

_____

An exercise during which the fingers of the child are enumerated.

Tʜᴜᴍʙɪᴋɪɴ, Thumbikin, broke the barn,
Pinnikin, Pinnikin, stole the corn.
Long backed Gray
Carried it away.
Old Mid-man sat and saw,
But Peesy-weesy paid for a'.

_____

A GAME ON THE FINGERS.

Hᴇᴇᴛᴜᴍ peetum penny pie,
Populorum gingum gie;
East, West, North, South,
Kirby, Kendal, cock him out!

THE two following are fragments of a game called "The Lady of the Land."

Here comes a poor woman from Baby-land,
With three small children in her hand:
One can brew, the other can bake,
The other can make a pretty round cake.
One can sit in the garden and spin,
Another can make a fine bed for the King;
Pray, ma'am, will you take one in?

THE first day of Christmas,
My true love sent to me
A partridge in a pear-tree.

The second day of Christmas,
My true love sent to me
Two turtle-doves and
A partridge in a pear-tree.

The third day of Christmas,
My true love sent to me
Three French hens,
Two turtle-doves, and
A partridge in a pear-tree.

The fourth day of Christmas,
My true love sent to me
Four colly birds,
Three French hens,
Two turtle-doves, and
A partridge in a pear-tree.

The fifth day of Christmas,
My true love sent to me
Five gold rings,
Four colly birds,
Three French hens,
Two turtle-doves, and
A partridge in a pear-tree.

The sixth day of Christmas,
My true love sent to me
Six geese a-laying,
Five gold rings,
Four colly birds,
Three French hens,
Two turtle-doves, and
A partridge in a pear-tree.

The seventh day of Christmas,
My true love sent to me
Seven swans a-swimming,
Six geese a-laying,

Five gold rings,
Four colly birds,
Three French hens,
Two turtle-doves, and
A partridge in a pear-tree.

The eighth day of Christmas,
My true love sent to me
Eight maids a-milking,
Seven swans a-swimming,
Six geese a-laying,
Five gold rings,
Four colly birds,
Three French hens,
Two turtle-doves, and
A partridge in a pear-tree.

The ninth day of Christmas,
My true love sent to me
Nine drummers drumming,
Eight maids a-milking,
Seven swans a-swimming,
Six geese a-laying,
Five gold rings,
Four colly birds,
Three French hens,
Two turtle-doves, and
A partridge in a pear-tree.

The tenth day of Christmas,
My true love sent to me
Ten pipers piping,

Nine drummers drumming,
Eight maids a-milking,
Seven swans a-swimming,
Six geese a-laying,
Five gold rings,
Four colly birds,
Three French hens,
Two turtle doves, and
A partridge in a pear-tree.

The eleventh day of Christmas,
My true love sent to me
Eleven ladies dancing,
Ten pipers piping,
Nine drummers drumming,
Eight maids a-milking,
Seven swans a-swimming,
Six geese a-laying,
Five gold rings,
Four colly birds,
Three French hens,
Two turtle-doves, and
A partridge in a pear-tree.

The twelfth day of Christmas
My true love sent to me
Twelve lords a-leaping,
Eleven ladies dancing,
Ten pipers piping,
Nine drummers drumming,

Eight maids a-milking,
Seven swans a-swimming,
Six geese a-laying,
Five gold rings,

Four colly birds,
Three French hens,
Two turtle-doves, and
A partridge in a pear-tree.

Each child in succession repeats the gifts of the day, and raises her fingers and hands according to the numbers named. Forfeits are paid for each mistake.

This accumulative process is a favorite one with children. In early writers, such as Homer, the repetition of messages, &c., pleases on the same principle.

THE POOR SOLDIER.

CHILDREN form a half-circle, first choosing one of their number to represent the poor soldier. The chief regulation is that none of the players may use the words "yes," "no," "black," "white," or "grey." The poor soldier traverses the semicircle thus addressing each player:

" Here's a poor soldier come to town!
Have you aught to give him ?"

The answer must, of course, be evasive, else there is a fine. He continues, " Have you a pair of trousers [or old coat, shoes, cap, &c] to give me?" The answer must again be evasive, or else another forfeit. The old soldier then asks, " Well, what color is it ?" The reply must avoid the forbidden colors, or another forfeit is the penalty. Great ingenuity may be exhibited in the manner in which the questions and answers are constructed, and in the hands of some children, this is a most amusing recreation. The forfeits are, of course, cried at the end of the game.

THE DIAMOND RING.

CHILDREN sit in a ring or in a line, with their hands placed together palm to palm, and held straight, the little fingers downmost between the knees. One of them is then chosen to represent a servant, who conceals a ring, or some other small article as a substitute, in her hands, which are pressed flat together like those of the rest, and goes round the circle or line, placing her hands into the hands of every player, so that she is enabled to let the ring fall wherever she pleases without detection. After this, she returns to the first child she touched, and, with her hands behind her, exclaims,

" My lady's lost her diamond ring;
I pitch upon you to find it!"

The child who is thus addressed must guess who has the ring, and the servant performs the same ceremony with each of the party. Those who guess right, escape; but the rest forfeit. Should any one in the ring exclaim, "I have it!" she also forfeits; nor must the servant make known who has the ring, until all have guessed, under the same penalty. The forfeits are afterwards cried as usual.

I CAN make diet bread,
  Thick and thin;
I can make diet bread,
  Fit for the King.

THE following lines are repeated by the nurse when sliding her hand down the child's face:

My mother and your mother
  Went over the way;
Said my mother to your mother,
  It's chop-a-nose day!

The following lines are said by the nurse when moving the child's foot up and down:

The dog of the kill*
He went to the mill
  To lick mill-dust,
The miller he came
With a stick on his back—
  Home, dog, home!
The foot behind,
  The foot before,
When he came to a stile,
  Thus he jumped o'er.

      * That is, a kiln.

SLATE GAMES.

ENTERTAINING puzzles or exercises upon the slate are generally great favorites with children. A great variety of them are current in the nursery, or rather were so some years ago. The story of the four rich men, the four poor men, and the pond, was one of these; the difficulty merely requiring a zigzag enclosure to enable it to be satisfactorily solved.

Once upon a time there was a pond lying upon common land, which was extremely commodious for fishing, bathing, and various other purposes. Not far from it lived four poor men, to whom it was of great service; and, farther off, there lived four rich men. The latter envied the poor men the use of the pond, and, as enclosure bills had not then come into fashion, they wished to invent an enclosure-wall which should shut out the poor men from the pond, although they lived so near it, and still give free access to the rich men, who resided at a greater distance. How was this done?

THE GAME OF DUMP.

A Boy's amusement in Yorkshire, in vogue about half a century ago, but now, I believe, nearly obsolete. It is played in this manner   The lads crowd round and place their fists endways the one on the other till they form a high pile of hands.   Then a boy who has one hand free, knocks the piled fists off one by one, saying to every boy as he strikes his fists away, "What's there, Dump?"   He continues this process till he comes to the last fist, when he exclaims,

What's there?—Cheese and bread and a moldy half-
    penny!

Where's my share ?—I put it on the shelf, and the cat
    got it.

Where's the cat ?—She's run nine miles through the
    wood.

Where's the wood ?—T' fire burnt it.
Where's the fire ?—T' water sleckt [extinguished] it.
Where's the water ?—T' oxen drunk it.
Where's the oxen ?—T' butcher kill'd 'em.
Where's the butcher ?
Upon the church-top cracking nuts, and you may go
and eat the shells; and *them as* speak first shall
have nine nips, nine scratches, and nine boxes over
the lug !

Every one then endeavors to refrain from speaking,
in spite of mutual nudges and grimaces, and he who
first allows a word to escape is punished by the others
in the various methods adopted by schoolboys. In
some places the game is played differently. The
children pile their fists in the manner described above,
then one, or sometimes all of them, sing,

I've built my house, I've built my wall:
I don't care where my chimneys fall !

The merriment consists in the bustle and confusion
occasioned by the rapid withdrawal of the hands

THIS game is now played as follows: A child hides
something in one hand, and then places both fists endways on each other, crying,

Handy-dandy riddledy ro,
Which will you have, high or low ?
Or sometimes the following distich :
Handy-dandy, Jack-a-dandy,
Which good hand will you have ?"

The party addressed either touches one hand, or
guesses in which one the article (whatever it may be) is
placed. If he guesses rightly, he wins its contents; if
wrongly, he loses an equivalent.

Some versions read "Handy-pandy" in the first of these, with another variation that would not now be tolerated. This is one of the oldest English games in existence, and appears to be alluded to in "Piers Ploughman," ed. Wright, p. 69:

> " Thanne wowede Wrong
> Wisdom ful yerne,
> To maken pees with his pens,
> Handy-dandy played."

GAME OF THE CAT.

THIS is another slate game, in which, by means of a tale and appropriate indications on the slate, a rude figure of a cat is delineated. It requires, however, some little ingenuity to accomplish it.

Tommy would once go to see his cousin Charles. [Here one draws T for Tommy, and C for Charles, forming the forehead, nose, and mouth of the cat.] But before he went, he would make walls to his house. [Here he draws lines from the arms of the T to its foot, forming the cheeks of the cat.] But then it smoked, and he would put chimneys to it. [Here he inserts two narrow triangles on each arm of the T, forming the ears of the cat.] But then it was so dark, he would put windows into it. [Here he draws a small circle under each arm of the T, forming the eyes.] Then to make it pretty, he would spread grass at the door. [Here he scratches lines at the foot of the T, representing the cat's whiskers.] Then away he went on his journey, but after a little while, down he fell. [Here he draws down a line a little way from the foot of the T.] But he soon climbed up again. [Here he draws a zigzag horizontally from the foot of the last line, and draws one up, forming with the last movement the first foot of the cat.] Then he walks along again, but soon falls down once more. [Here he draws a short horizontal line, and one downwards.] He soon, however, got up again, as before, &c. [The second leg is then formed, and by similar movements the four legs of the cat appear.] After thus falling down four times, Tommy determined to proceed more firmly, and climbing up, he walks along [the back of the cat] another way round till he comes to C. His journey is now accomplished, and an animal, called by courtesy a cat, appears on the slate, "the admiration of all beholders."

THE OLD GAME OF HONEY-POTS.

ONE of the players must be selected to act the part of a Honey Merchant, another to come as a Purchaser to the honey stores. These two should be the tallest and strongest of the party.

The rest of the party represent pots of honey. They must clasp their hands under their raised knees, sitting in a row on the grass. Then the game proceeds thus:

The purchaser approaches the merchant and asks, "Have you any good honey for sale, friend?"

Honey Merchant. Yes, ma'am [or sir], first-rate. This pot is from Mount Hybla, the finest honey in the world; tastes of thyme, I assure you. This one is from Sicily, quite as good as any you would get at Fortnum and Mason's. Taste and try before you buy.

The purchaser goes round and pretends to taste the honey.

Purchaser (shaking his head). Not very good. I see that everything Greek is best *ancient.* Ah! I like this Sicilian jar. How much will you sell it for?

Honey Merchant. A shilling a pound.

Purchaser. What does the jar weigh?

Honey Merchant. We will see, sir, if you will be good enough to help me.

Then they take hold of the arms of the Sicilian jar

(who must hold her hands very tightly clasped under her knees), and swing her backwards and forwards till she is obliged to let her hands drop apart and her feet touch the ground. She is then said to weigh as many pounds as she has been times swung backwards and forwards.

Purchaser may object to the weight, and choose another pot; and thus the game goes on, till each jar has had a swing, and taken part in the sport.

GAME OF THE FOX.

ONE child is Fox. He has a knotted handkerchief, and a home to which he may go whenever he is tired; but while out of home he must always hop on one leg. The other children are Geese, and have no home. When the fox is coming out he says,

> The fox gives warning
> It's a cold frosty morning.

After he has said these words he is at liberty to hop out, and use his knotted handkerchief. Whoever he can touch is fox instead; but the geese run on two legs; and if the fox puts his other leg down, he is hunted back to his home.

ELEVENTH CLASS.
Paradoxes.

In a cottage in Fife
Lived a man and his wife,
Who, believe me, were comical folk;
For to people's surprise,
They both saw with their eyes,
And their tongues moved whenever they spoke!

When quite fast asleep,
I've been told that, to keep
Their eyes open they scarce could contrive:
They walked on their feet,
And 't was thought what they eat
Helped, with drinking, to keep them alive!!

The following is quoted in Parkin's reply to Dr. Stukeley's second number of "Origines Roystonianæ," 4to, London, 1748, p. vi.

PETER WHITE will ne'er go right:
Would you know the reason why?
He follows his nose where'er he goes,
And that stands all awry.

O THAT I was where I would be,
Then would I be where I am not!
But where I am I must be,
And where I would be, I cannot.

I SAW a ship a-sailing,
A-sailing on the sea;
And, oh! it was all laden
With pretty things for thee!

There were comfits in the cabin,
  And apples in the hold;
The sails were made of silk,
  And the masts were made of gold.

The four-and-twenty sailors
  That stood between the decks

Were four-and-twenty white mice,
With chains about their necks.

The captain was a duck,
With a packet on his back;
And when the ship began to move,
The captain said, "Quack! quack!"

I WOULD if I cou'd,
If I cou'dn't how cou'd I?
I cou'dn't, without I cou'd, cou'd I?
Cou'd you, without you cou'd, cou'd ye?
Cou'd ye, cou'd 'ye?
Cou'd you, without you cou'd, cou'd ye?

The following was sung to the tune of Chevy Chase. It was taken from a poetical tale in the "Choyce Poems," 12mo. London, 1662, the music to which may be seen in D'Urfey's "Pills to Purge Melancholy," 1719, Vol, IV., p. 1.

THREE children sliding on the ice
        Upon a summer's day,
    As it fell out they all fell in,
        The rest they ran away.

Now, had these children been at home,
Or sliding on dry ground,
Ten thousand pounds to one penny
They had not all been drowned.

You parents all that children have,
And you that have got none,
If you would have them safe abroad,
Pray keep them safe at home.

THERE was a little Guinea-pig,
Who, being little, was not big;
He always walked upon his feet,
And never fasted when he eat.

When from a place he ran away,
He never at that place did stay;
And while he ran, as I am told,
He ne'er stood still for young or old.

He often squeaked, and sometimes vi'lent,
And when he squeaked he ne'er was silent:
Though ne'er instructed by a cat,
He knew a mouse was not a rat.

One day, as I am certified,
He took a whim and fairly died;
And, as I'm told by men of sense,
He never has been living since!

I SAW a peacock with a fiery tail,
I saw a blazing comet drop down hail,
I saw a cloud wrapped with ivy round,
I saw an oak creep upon the ground,
I saw a pismire swallow up a whale,
I saw the sea brimful of ale.

I saw a Venice glass full fifteen feet deep,
I saw a well full of men's tears that weep,
I saw red eyes all of a flaming fire,
I saw a house bigger than the moon and higher,
I saw the sun at twelve o'clock at night,
I saw the man that saw this wondrous sight.

THERE was a man of Newington,
　　And he was wondrous wise,
He jumped into a quickset hedge,
　　And scratched out both his eyes;

But when he saw his eyes were out,
　　With all his might and main
He jumped into another hedge
　　And scratched 'em in again.

IF all the world was apple pie,
　　And all the sea was ink,
And all the trees were bread and cheese,
　　What should we have for drink?

The conclusion of the following resembles a verse in the nursery history of Mother Hubbard.

THERE was an old woman, and what do you think?
She lived upon nothing but victuals and drink:
Victuals and drink were the chief of her diet;
This tiresome old woman could never be quiet.

She went to the baker, to buy her some bread,
And when she came home her old husband was dead;
She went to the clerk to toll the bell,
And when she came back her old husband was well.

THE man in the wilderness asked me,
How many strawberries grew in the sea?
I answered him as I thought good,
As many as red herrings grew in the wood.

THERE was a man and he
   was mad,
And he jumped into a pea-
   swad;

The pea-swad was over-
   full,
So he jumped into a roar-
   ing bull;

The roaring bull was over-fat,
So he jumped into a gentleman's hat;

The gentleman's hat was over-fine,
So he jumped into a bottle of wine;
The bottle of wine was over-dear,
So he jumped into a barrel of beer;
The barrel of beer was over-thick,
So he jumped into a club-stick;

The club-stick was over-narrow,
So he jumped into a wheelbarrow;
The wheelbarrow began to crack,
So he jumped on to a hay-stack;
The hay-stack began to blaze,
So he did nothing but cough and sneeze!

THERE was an old woman had nothing,
    And there came thieves to rob her;
When she cried out she made no noise,
    But all the country heard her.

UP stairs, down stairs, upon my lady's window,
There I saw a cup of sack and a race of ginger;
Apples at the fire and nuts to crack,
A little boy in the cream-pot up to his neck.

TOBACCO wick! tobacco wick!
When you're well, 'twill make you sick;
Tobacco wick! tobacco wick!
'Twill make you well when you are sick.

BARNEY BODKIN broke his nose,
Without feet we can't have toes;
Crazy folks are always mad,
Want of money makes us sad.

IF a man who turnips cries
Cries not when his father dies,
It is a proof that he would rather
Have a turnip than his father.

My true love lives far from me,
  Perrie, Merrie, Dixie, Dominie.
Many a rich present he sends to me,
    Petrum, Partrum, Paradise Temporie.
    Perrie, Merrie, Dixie, Dominie.
He sent me a goose without a bone;
He sent me a cherry without a stone.
                    Petrum, &c.
He sent me a Bible no man could read;
He sent me a blanket without a thread.
                    Petrum, &c.
How could there be a goose without a bone?
How could there be a cherry without a stone?
                    Petrum, &c.
How could there be a Bible no man could read?
How could there be a blanket without a thread?
                    Petrum, &c.
When the goose is in the egg-shell, there is no bone;
When the cherry is in the blossom, there is no stone.
                    Petrum, &c.
When y^e Bible is in y^e press, no man it can read;
When y^e wool is on y^e sheep's back, there is no thread.
                    Petrum, &c.

Here am I
  Little jumping loan;
When nobody's with me,
  I'm always alone.

TWELFTH CLASS.
Lullabies.

ROCK-A-BYE, baby, thy cradle is green;
Father's a nobleman, mother's a Queen;
And Betty's a lady, and wears a gold ring!
And Johnny's a drummer, and drums for the King.

———

RIDE, baby, ride,
Pretty baby shall ride,
And have a little puppy-dog tied
to her side,
And little pussy-cat tied to the
other,
And away she shall ride to see her
grandmother,
To see her grandmother,
To see her grandmother.

From "The Pleasant Comœdie of Patient Grissell," 1603.

HUSH, hush, hush, hush!
And I dance mine own child,
And I dance mine own child,
Hush, hush, hush, hush!

Bye, baby bunting,
Daddy's gone a-hunt-
ing,
To get a little hare's
skin
To wrap a baby bunt-
ing in.

Give me a blow, and
I'll beat 'em,
Why did they vex
my baby?
Kissy, kiss, kissy, my
honey,
And cuddle your
nurse, my deary.

Tom shall have a new bonnet,
With blue ribbons to tie on it,
With a hush-a-bye and a lull-a-baby,
Why so like to Tommy's daddy?

My dear cockadoodle, my jewel, my joy,
My darling, my honey, my pretty sweet boy;
Before I do rock thee with soft lullaby,
Give me thy dear lips to be kissed, kissed, kissed.

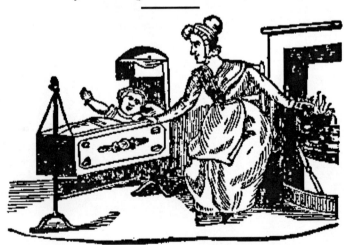

Bye, O my baby!
When I was a lady,
Oh, then my poor baby
didn't cry.

But my baby is weeping
For want of good keeping,
Oh, I fear my poor baby
will die!

Hey, my kitten, my kitten,
  And hey, my kitten, my deary!
Such a sweet pet as this
  Was neither far nor neary.

Here we go up, up, up,
  And here we go down, down, downy,
And here we go backwards and forwards,
  And here we go round, round, roundy.

Rock well my cradle,
  And "bee baa," my son;
You shall have a new gown
  When y^e lord comes home.

Oh! still my child, Orange,
  Still him with a bell;
I can't still him, ladie,
  Till you come down yourself!

Hush-a-bye, baby, on the tree-top,
When the wind blows the cradle will rock;
When the bough bends the cradle will fall,
Down will come baby, bough, cradle, and all.

Hush-a-bye, a ba lamb,
　Hush-a-bye a milk cow,
You shall have a little stick
　To beat the naughty
　bowwow.

Bye, baby bumpkin,
Where's Tony Lumpkin?
My lady's on her death-bed,
With eating half a pump-
　kin.

Hush thee, my babby,
Lie still with thy daddy,
Thy mammy has gone to the mill
To grind thee some wheat,
To make thee some meat,
And so, my dear babby, lie still.

Dance to your daddy,
My little babby,
Dance to your daddy,
My little lamb.

You shall have a fishy
In a little dishy;
You shall have a fishy
When the boat comes in.

From Yorkshire.   A nursery cry.

RABBIT, rabbit, rabbit pie!
Come, my ladies, come and buy;
Else your babies they will cry.

———

I won't be my father's Jack,
    I won't be my mother's Gill,
I will be the fiddler's wife,
    And have music when I will.
        T' other little tune,
        T' other little tune,
        Pr'ythee, love, play me
        T' other little tune.

From Yorkshire and Essex. A nursery cry. It is also sometimes sung in the streets by boys who have small figures of wool, wood, or gypsum, &c., of lambs to sell.

> Young Lambs to sell!
> Young Lambs to sell!
> If I'd as much money as I can tell,
> I never would cry—Young Lambs to sell!

> Danty baby diddy,
> What can a mammy do wid'e,
>   But sit in a lap,
>   And give 'un a pap?
> Sing danty, baby diddy.

A favorite lullaby in the North of England fifty years ago, and perhaps still heard. The last word is pronounced *bee*.

HUSH-A-BYE, lie still and
sleep,
It grieves me sore to see
thee weep,
For when thou weep'st
thou wearies me,
Hush-a-bye, lie still and
bye.

DANCE, little baby, dance
up high,
Never mind, baby, mother
is by;
Crow and caper, caper and
crow,
There, little baby, there
you go;
Up to the ceiling, down to
the ground,
Backwards and forwards,
round and round;
Dance, little baby, and
mother will sing,
With the merry coral,
ding, ding, ding!

To market, to market,
To buy a plum cake.
Home again, home again,
Ne'er a one baked;
The baker is dead and all his men,
And we must go to market again.

Hushy baby, my doll, I pray you don't cry,
And I'll give you some bread and some milk by-and-bye;
Or perhaps you like custard, or maybe a tart,—
Then to either you're welcome, with all my whole heart.

The following is quoted in Florio's
"New World of Words," fol., London,
1611, p. 3.

To market, to market,
   To buy a plum bun;
Home again, come again,
   Market is done.

THIRTEENTH CLASS.

Jingles.

Hey ding a ding, what shall I sing?
How many holes in a skimmer?
Four and twenty,—my stomach is empty;
Pray, mamma, give me some dinner.

The first line of the following is the burden of a song in the "Tempest," Act 1. sc. 2, and also of one in the "Merchant of Venice," Act III. sc. 2.

DING, dong bell,
Pussy's in the well.
Who put her in?

Little Tommy Lin.
Who pulled her out?—
Dog with long snout.

What a naughty boy was that
To drown poor pussy-cat,
Who never did any harm,
But killed the mice in his father's barn.

———

Sing jigmijole, the pudding-bowl,
The table and the frame;
My master he did cudgel me
For speaking of my dame.

———

Deedle, deedle, dumpling, my son John
Went to bed with his trowsers on;
One shoe off, the other shoe on,
Deedle, deedle, dumpling, my son John.

———

Diddledy, diddledy,
dumpty:
The cat ran up the plum-
tree.
I'll lay you a crown
I'll fetch you down;
So diddledy, diddledy,
dumpty.

———

See-saw, Jack in a hedge,
Which is the way to London Bridge?
One foot up, the other down,
That is the way to London town.

———

Hey diddle, dinketty, poppety, pet,
The merchants of London they wear scarlet;
Silk in the collar, and gold in the hem,
So merrily march the merchantmen.

Sing, sing, what shall I sing?
The cat has ate the pudding-string!
Do, do, what shall I do?
The cat has bit it quite in two.

I do not know whether the following may have reference to the game of handy-dandy mentioned in "King Lear," Act IV. sc. 6, and in Florio's "New World of Words," 1611, p. 57.

HANDY Spandy, Jack-a-dandy,
Loved plum cake and sugar-candy;
He bought some at a grocer's shop,
And out he came, hop, hop, hop.

HYDER iddle diddle dell,
A yard of pudding is not an ell;
Not forgetting tweddle-dye,
A tailor's goose will never fly.

GILLY Silly Jarter,
Who has lost a garter,
In a shower of rain?
The miller found it,
The miller ground it,
And the miller gave it to
Silly again.

FEEDUM, fiddledum fee,
The cat's got into the tree.
Pussy, come down,
Or I'll crack your crown,
And toss you into the sea.

Dibbity, dibbity, dibbity,
    doe,
Give me a pancake
    And I'll go.

Dibbity dibbity, dibbity,
    ditter,
Please to give me
    A bit of a fritter.

Tweedle-dum and Tweedle-dee
    Resolved to have a battle,
For Tweedle-dum said Tweedle-dee
    Had spoiled his nice new rattle.
Just then flew by a monstrous crow,
    As big as a tar-barrel,
Which frightened both the heroes so,
    They quite forgot their quarrel.

Hub a dub dub,
    Three men in a tub;
And who do you think
    they be?

The butcher, the baker,
    The candlestick maker;
Turn 'em out knaves all
    three!

Tiddle liddle lightum,
    Pitch and tar:

Tiddle liddle lightum,
    What's that for?

HIGH, ding, cockatoo-moody,
Make a bed in a barn, I will come to thee;
High ding, straps of leather,
Two little puppy-dogs tied together;
One by the head, and one by the tail,
And over the water these puppy-dogs sail.

DOODLEDY, doodledy, doodledy, dan,
I'll have a piper to be my good man;
And if I get less meat, I shall get game,
Doodledy, doodledy, doodledy, dan.

LITTLE Tee Wee,   And while afloat
He went to sea   The little boat bended,
In an open boat;   And my story's ended.

FIDDLE-DE-DEE, fiddle-de-dee,
The fly shall marry the humble-bee.
They went to the church, and married was she,
The fly has married the humble-bee.

DOODLE doodle doo,   The fiddler stopped,
The Princess lost her shoe;   Not knowing what to do.
  Her Highness hopped,—

PUSSICAT, wussicat, with a white foot,
When is your wedding? for I'll come to 't.
The beer's to brew, the bread's to bake,
Pussy-cat, pussy-cat, don't be too late.

ROMPTY iddity, row, row, row,
If I had a good supper, I could eat it now.

COME, dance a jig
  To my granny's pig,
With a raudy, rowdy,
    dowdy;
  Come dance a jig
  To my granny's pig,
And pussy-cat shall crowdy.

HICKETY, dickety, dock,
The mouse ran up the
  clock;
  The clock struck one,
  Down the mouse ran,
Hickety, dickety, dock.

———

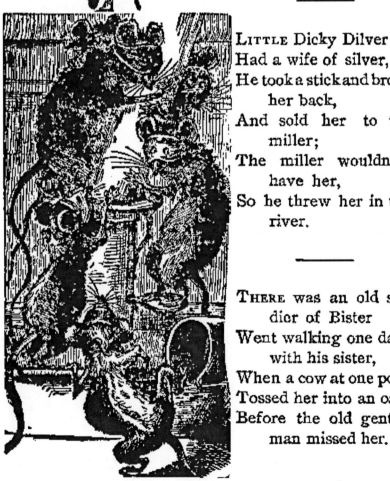

LITTLE Dicky Dilver
Had a wife of silver,
He took a stick and broke
  her back,
And sold her to the
  miller;
The miller wouldn't
  have her,
So he threw her in the
  river.

———

THERE was an old sol-
  dier of Bister
Went walking one day
  with his sister,
When a cow at one poke
Tossed her into an oak,
Before the old gentle-
  man missed her.

A CAT came fiddling out of a barn,
With a pair of bagpipes under her arm;
She could sing nothing but fiddle cum fee,
The mouse has married the bumble-bee!
Pipe, cat; dance, mouse:
We'll have a wedding at our good house.

OLD woman, old woman, shall we go a-shearing?
Speak a little louder, sir,—I am very thick of hearing.
Old woman, old woman, shall I love you dearly?
Thank you, kind sir. I hear you very clearly.

THERE was an old woman, her name it was Peg;
Her head was of wood, and she wore a cork leg.
The neighbors all pitched her into the water,
Her leg was drowned first, and her head followed a'ter,

LITTLE Polly Flinders,
Sat among the cinders,
  Warming her pretty toes;
Her mother came and caught her,
And scolded her little daughter,
  For spoiling her nice new clothes,

THERE was an old woman who lived in a
    shoe,
She had so many children she didn't know
    what to do;
She gave them some broth without any
    bread,
She whipped them all well and put them
    to bed.

LITTLE Jack a Dandy
Wanted sugar-can-
    dy,
And fairly for it
    cried;
But little Billy Cook,
Who always reads
    his book,
  Shall have a horse
    to ride.

Hey! diddle diddle,
The cat and the fiddle,
The cow jumped over the moon;
The little dog laughed
To see the sport,
While the dish ran after the spoon.

Hey, dorolot, dorolot!
  Hey, dorolay, dorolay!
Hey, my bonny boat, bonny boat,
  Hey, drag away, drag away!

THERE was an old woman sat spinning,
And that's the first beginning;
She had a calf, and that's half;

She took it by the tail,
And threw it over the wall,
And that's all.

DING, dong, darrow,
The cat and the sparrow;
The little dog has burnt his tail,
And he shall be hanged to-morrow.

Magotty-pie is given in MS. Lands 1033, fol. 2, as a Wiltshire word for a magpie. See also "Macbeth," Act III. sc. 4. The same term occurs in the dictionaries of Hollyband, Cotgrave, and Minsheu.

Round about, round about,   My father loves good ale,
   Magotty-pie,   And so do I.

Cock a doodle doo!
My dame has lost her shoe;
My master's lost his fiddling-stick,
And don't know what to do.

Cock a doodle doo!
What is my dame to do?
Till master finds his fiddling-stick,
She'll dance without her shoe.

Cock a doodle doo!
My dame has lost her shoe,
And master's found his fiddling-stick,
Sing doodle doodle doo!

Cock a doodle doo!
My dame will dance with you,
While master fiddles his fiddling-stick,
For dame and doodle doo.

Cock a doodle doo!
Dame has lost her shoe;
Gone to bed and scratched her head.
And can't tell what to do.

OLD Dame Widdle Wad-
dle
Jumped out of bed,
And out at the casement
She popped her head,
Crying, The house is on
fire,
The grey goose dead
And the fox he is
Come to town, oh!

"FIRE! fire!" said the town crier;
"Where? where?" said Goody Blair;
"Down the town," said Goody Brown;
"I'll go and see 't" said Goody Fleet;
"So will I," said Goody Fry.

To market, to market, to buy a fat pig,
Home again, home again, dancing a jig;
Ride to the market to buy a fat hog,
Home again, home again, jiggety-jog.

Is John Smith within?   Here a nail and there a
Yes, that he is.   nail,
Can he set a shoe?   Tick, tack, too.
Ay, marry, two;

Our collection of nursery jingles may appropriately be concluded with the Quaker's commentary on one of the greatest favorites—"Hey! diddle diddle." We have endeavored, as far as practicable, to remove every line from the present addition that could offend the most fastidious ear; but the following annotations on a song we cannot be induced to omit, would appear to suggest that our endeavors are scarcely likely to be attended with success.

HEY! diddle diddle,
The cat and the fiddle—

"Yes, thee may say that, for that is nonsense."

The cow jumped over the moon—

"Oh no! Mary, thee mustn't say that, for that is a falsehood; thee knows a cow could never jump over the moon; but a cow may jump under it; so thee ought to say—'The cow jumped *under* the moon.'"
Yes,—

The cow jumped under the moon;
The little dog laughed—

"Oh, Mary, stop. How can a little dog laugh? thee knows a little dog can't laugh. Thee ought to say—'The little dog *barked*'"—

To see the sport,
And the dish ran after the spoon—

"Stop, Mary, stop. A dish could never run after a spoon; thee ought to know that. Thee had better say—'And the *cat* ran after the spoon,'" So,—

Hey! diddle diddle,
The cat and the fiddle,
The cow jumped *under* the moon.
The little dog *barked*
To see the sport,
And the *cat* ran after the spoon.

FOURTEENTH CLASS.

Natural History.

THE cuckoo's a fine bird,
　He sings as he flies;
He brings us good tidings,
　He tells us no lies.

He sucks little birds' eggs,
　To make his voice clear,
And when he sings
　　　　"cuckoo!"
The summer is near.

A provincial version of the same.

THE cuckoo's a vine bird,
　A zengs as a vlies;
A brengs us good tidins,
　And tells us no lies;
A zucks th' smael birds' eggs,
　To make his voice clear;
And the mwore a cries
　　"cuckoo!"
The zummer draws near.

Cuckoo, Cuckoo,
What do you do?
In April
I open my bill;
In May
I sing night and day;
In June
I change my tune;
In July
Away I fly;
In August
Away I must.

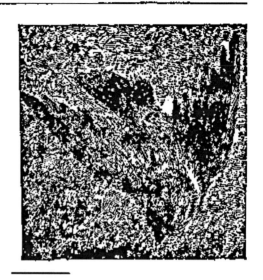

In the month of February,
    When green leaves begin to spring,
Little lambs do skip like fairies,
    Birds do couple, build, and sing.

See-Saw, Margery Daw,
    The old hen flew over the malt-house;
She counted her chickens one by one,
Still she missed the little white one,
And this is it, this is it, this is it!

I'll away yhame,
And tell my dame
That all my geese
Are gane but yane;

And it's a steg (*gander*),
And it's lost a leg;
And it'll be gane
By I yet yhame.

Jack Spratt
Had a cat,
It had but one ear;

It went to buy butter,
When butter was dear.

———

Pretty John Watts,
We are troubled with rats,
Will you drive them out of
    the house?
We have mice, too, in
    plenty,
That feast in the pantry;
But let them stay,
And nibble away:
What harm in a little brown
    mouse?

How d' 'e, dogs, how! whose dog art thou?
Little Tom Tinker's dog! what's that to thou?
Hiss! bow, a wow, wow!

The Proverb of Barnaby Bright is given by Ray and Brand as referring to St. Barnabas.

BARNABY Bright he was a sharp
    cur,
He always would bark. if a
    mouse did but stir;
But now he's grown old, and
    can no longer bark,
He's condemned by the parson
    to be hanged by the clerk.

LITTLE boy blue, come blow
    your horn,
The sheep's in the meadow, the
    cow's in the corn.
Where's the little boy that looks
    after the sheep?
He's under the haycock fast
    asleep.
Will you wake him? No, not I;
For if I do, he'll be sure to cry.

Bow, wow, says the dog;
　Mew, mew, says the cat;
Grunt, grunt, goes the hog;
　And squeak goes the rat.

Tu-whu, says the owl;
　Caw, caw, says the crow.
Quack, quack, says the
　　duck;
　And what sparrows say,
　　you know.

So, with sparrows and owls,
　With rats and with dogs,
With ducks and with crows,
　With cats and with hogs,

A fine song I have made,
　To please you, my dear;
And if it's well sung,
　'T will be charming to
　　hear.

Leg over leg,
As the dog went to
　Dover;
When he came to a
　stile,
Jump! he went over.

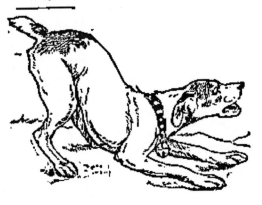

Rowsty dowt, my fire's all out,
My little dame is not at home!
I'll saddle my cock, and bridle my hen,
And fetch my little dame home again!
Home she came, tritty trot,
She asked for the porridge she left in the pot;
Some she ate and some she shod,
And some she gave to the truckler's dog;
She took up the ladle and knocked its head,
And now poor Dapsy dog is dead!

Goosey, goosey, gan-
der,
Where shall I wander?
Upstairs, downstairs,
And in my lady's
chamber;
There I met an old man
That would not say
his prayers;
I took him by the left
leg,
And threw him down-
stairs.

Goosey, goosey, gander, Little Betsy Baker;
Who stands yonder ? Take her up, and shake her.

Hurly Burly, trumpet trase,
The cow was in the market-place,
Some goes far, and some goes near,
But where shall this poor henchman steer ?

Riddle me, riddle me, ree,
A hawk sate up on a tree;
And he says to himself, says he,
Oh dear! what a fine bird I be!

THE sow came in with the saddle,
The little pig rocked the cradle,
The dish jumped over the table,
To see the pot with the ladle.
The broom behind the butt
Called the dish-clout a nasty slut:
Oh! oh! says the gridiron, can't you agree?
I'm the head constable—come along with me.

PUSSY-CAT sits by the fire:
How did she come there?
In walks the little dog—
Says, "Pussy! are you there?
How do you do, Mistress Pussy?
Mistress Pussy, how d'ye do?"
"I thank you kindly, little dog,
I fare as well as you!"

Hussy, hussy, where's your horse?
Hussy, hussy, gone to grass!
Hussy, hussy, fetch him home,
Hussy, hussy, let him alone.

"WHAT do they call you?" "Where were you bred?"
"Patchy Dolly." "In the cow's head."
"Where were you born?" "Where will you die?"
"In the cow's horn." "In the cow's eye."

SNAIL, snail, shoot out your horns;
   Father and mother are dead:
Brother and sister are in the back yard,
   Begging for barley bread.

Bird-boy's Song.

EAT, birds, eat, and make no waste,
I lie here and make no haste;
If my master chance to come,
You must fly, and I must run.

THE cat sat asleep by the side of the
   fire,
The mistress snored loud as a pig:
Jack took up his fiddle, by Jenny's
         desire,
     And struck up a bit
       of a jig.

ON Christmas Eve I turned the spit,
I burnt my fingers, I feel it yet.
The cock-sparrow flew over the table.
The pot began to play with the ladle.

ROBIN-A-BOBBIN bent his bow,
And shot at a woodcock and killed a yowe:
The yowe cried ba, and he ran away,
And never came back till Midsummer Day.

A LONG-TAILED, pig, or a   A sow-pig, or a boar-pig,
   short-tailed pig,   Or a pig with a curly tail.
Or a pig without e'er a tail,

LADYBIRD, ladybird, fly away home,
   Thy house is on fire, thy children all gone,
   All but one, and her name is Ann,
   And she crept under the pudding-pan.

Why is pussy in bed, pray?
   She is sick says the fly,
   And I fear she will die;
That's why she's in bed.

Pray, what's her disorder?
   She's got a locked jaw,
   Says the little jackdaw,
And that's her disorder.

Who makes her gruel?
   I, says the horse,
   For I am her nurse,
And I make her gruel.

Pray, who is her doctor ?
   Quack, quack! says the
     duck,
   I that task undertook,
And I am her doctor.

Who thinks she'll recover?
   I, says the deer,
   For I did last year:
So I think she'll recover.

Catch him, crow! carry him, kite!
Take him away till the apples are ripe;
When they are ripe and ready to fall,
Home comes [Johnny], apples and all.

An ancient Suffolk song for a bad singer.

THERE was an old crow There's an end of my song,
 Sat upon a clod: That's odd!

I HAD a little dog, and his name was Blue Bell,
I gave him some work, and he did it very well;
I sent him upstairs to pick up a pin,
He stepped in the coal-scuttle up to the chin;

I sent him to the garden to pick some sage,
He tumbled down and fell in a rage;
I sent him to the cellar to draw a pot of beer,
He came up again and said there was none there.

Bah, bah, black sheep,
  Have you any wool?
Yes, marry, have I,
  Three bags full;

One for my master,
  And one for my dame,
But none for the little boy
  Who cries in the lane.

I LIKE little pussy, her coat is so warm,
And if I don't hurt her she'll do me no harm;
So I'll not pull her tail, nor drive her away,
But pussy and I very gently will play.

I HAD a little hobby-horse, and it was well shod,
It carried me to the mill-door, trod, trod, trod;
When I got there I gave a great shout,
Down came the hobby-horse, and I cried out.
Fie upon the miller! he was a great beast,
He would not come to my house, I made a little feast:
I had but little, but I would give him some,
For playing of his bagpipes and beating his drum.

The Cock.   LOCK the dairy door,
               Lock the dairy door!
The Hen.   Chickle, chackle, chee,
               I have'nt got the key!

Imitated from a pigeon.

CURR dhoo, curr dhoo,
Love me, and I'll love you!

Bow, wow, wow,
  Whose dog art thou?
Little Tom Tinker's
  dog,
Bow, wow, wow.

PITTY Patty Polt,
Shoe the wild colt!

Here a nail, and there a
  nail,
Pitty Patty Polt.

LITTLE Robin Redbreast
  Sat upon a rail:
Niddle naddle went his head,
  Wiggle waggle went his tail.

LITTLE Robin Redbreast sat upon a tree,
Up went pussy-cat, and down went he;
Down came pussy-cat, and away Robin ran;
Says little Robin Redbreast, "Catch me if you can."

Little Robin Redbreast jumped upon a wall,
Pussy-cat jumped after him, and almost got a fall;

Little Robin chirped and sang, and what did pussy say?
Pussy-cat said "Mew," and Robin jumped away.

LITTLE Cock Robin peeped out of his cabin,
To see the cold winter come in,
　　Tit for tat, what matter for that?
　　He'll hide his head under his wing!

THE dove says coo, coo, what shall I do?
I can scarce maintain two.
Pooh, pooh, says the wren, I have got ten,
And keep them all like gentlemen!

A LITTLE cock sparrow sat on a green tree, *(tris)*
And he chirruped, he chirruped, so merry was he; *(tris)*
A little cock sparrow sat on a green tree,
And he chirruped, he chirruped, so merry was he.
A naughty boy came with his wee bow and arrow, *(tris)*
Determined to shoot this little cock sparrow, *(tris)*
　　　　A naughty boy, &c.
　　　　Determined, &c.
This little cock sparrow shall make me a stew, *(tris)*
And his giblets shall make me a little pie too; *(tris)*
Oh, no! said the sparrow, I *won't* make a stew,
So he flapped his wings and away he flew!

I HAD a little pony,
  His name was Dapple-gray,
I lent him to a lady,
  To ride a mile away;

She whipped him, she slashed him,
  She rode him through the mire;

I would not lend my pony now
For all the lady's hire.

Come hither, sweet robin,
    And be not afraid,
  I would not hurt even a feather;
Come hither, sweet Robin,
    And pick up some bread,
  To feed you this very cold weather.

I don't mean to frighten you,
    Poor little thing,
  And pussy-cat is not behind me;
So hop about pretty,
    And drop down your wing,
  And pick up some crumbs,
    And don't mind me.

THERE was an owl lived in an oak,
   Wisky, wasky, weedle;
And every word he ever spoke
   Was fiddle, faddle, feedle.

A gunner chanced to come that way,
   Wisky, wasky, weedle;
Says he, "I'll shoot you, silly bird,"
   Fiddle, faddle, feedle

The following song is given in Whiter's "Specimen, or a Commentary on Shakspeare," 8 vo, London, 1794, p. 19, as common in Cambridgeshire and Norfolk. Dr. Farmer gives another version as an illustration of a ditty of Jacques in "As You Like It," Act II. sc. 5. See Malone's Shakspeare, ed. 1821, Vol. VI. p. 398; Caldecott's "Specimen," 1819, note on "As You Like It," p. 11; and Douce's "Illustrations," Vol. I. p. 297.

Dame, what makes your ducks to die?
What the pize ails 'em? what the pize ails 'em?
They kick up their heels, and there they lie,
What the pize ails 'em now?
Heigh, ho! heigh, ho!
Dame, what makes your ducks to die?
What a pize ails 'em? what a pize ails 'em
Heigh, ho! heigh, ho!
Dame, what ails your ducks to die?
Eating o' polly-wigs, eating o' polly-wigs,
Heigh, ho! heigh, ho!

The pettitoes are little feet,
And the little feet not big;
Great feet belong to the grunting hog,
And the pettitoes to the little pig.

There was a little boy went into a barn,
And lay down on some hay;
An owl came out and flew about,
And the little boy ran away.

WILLYWITE, Willywite,　　　If he's not gone,
　　With his long bill;　　　　He stands there still

LITTLE Poll Parrot
Sat in his garret,
Eating toast and tea;
　A little brown mouse,
　Jumped into the house,
And stole it all away.

The snail scoops out hollows, little rotund chambers, in limestone, for its residence.　This habit of the animal is so important in its effects, as to have attracted the attention of geologists, and Dr. Buckland alluded to it at the meeting of the British Association in 1841.—The following rhyme is a boy's invocation to the snail to come out of such holes.

SNAIL, snail, come out of your
　　hole,
Or else I will beat you as black
　　as a coal.

SNAIL, snail, put out your horns,
I'll give you bread and barley-
　　corns.

Sneel, snaul,
Robbers are coming to pull down your wall;
Sneel, snaul,
Put out your horn,
Robbers are coming to steal your corn,
Coming at four o'clock in the morn.

All of a row,　Shot at a pigeon,
Bend the bow,　And killed a crow.

Pit, pat, well-a-day!
Little Robin flew away;
Where can little Robin be?
Gone into the cherry-tree.

When the snow is on the ground,
Little Robin Redbreast grieves,
For no berries can be found,
And on the trees there are no leaves.

The air is cold, the worms are hid;
For this poor bird what can be done?
We'll strew him here some crumbs of bread,
And then he'll live till the snow is gone.

A pye sate on a pear-tree,
A pye sate on a pear-tree,
A pye sate on a pear-tree,
Heigh O! heigh O! heigh O!
Once so merrily hopp'd she,
Twice so merrily hopp'd she,
Thrice so merrily hopp'd she,
Heigh O! heigh O! heigh O!

Cock Robin got up early
 At the break of day,
And went to Jenny's win-
  dow
 To sing a roundelay.

He sang Cock Robin's love
 To the pretty Jenny
  Wren,
And when he got unto the
  end,
 Then he began again.

Pussy-cat, pussy-cat, where have you been?
I've been to London to look at the Queen.
Pussy-cat, pussy-cat, what did you there?
I frightened a little mouse under the chair.

A Dorsetshire version of the "Four-and-Twenty Tailors."

'T was the twenty-ninth of May, 't was a holiday,
Four-and-twenty tailors set out to hunt a snail;
The snail put forth his horns, and roared like a bull,
Away ran the tailors, and catch the snail who wull.

 The Robin and the wren
 They fought upon the parrage-pan;
 But ere the Robin got a spoon,
 The wren had ate the parrage down.

Little Bob Robin,
Where do you live?

Up in yonder wood, sir,
On a hazel twig.

I HAD a little hen, the prettiest ever seen,
She washed me the dishes and kept the house clean;
She went to the mill to fetch me some flour,
She brought it home in less than an hour;
She baked me my bread, she brewed me my ale,
She sat by the fire and told many a fine tale.

A north of England version of a very common nursery rhyme, sung by a
child, who imitates the crowing of a cock.

COCK-A-DOODLE-DOO,
My dad's gane to ploo;
Mammy's lost her pudding-poke,
And knows not what to do.

Higglepy piggleby, my black hen,
She lays eggs for gentlemen;
Sometimes nine, and sometimes ten,
Higglepy piggleby, my black hen!

Hickety, pickety, my black hen,
She lays eggs for gentlemen,
Gentlemen come every day
To see what my black hen doth
　　lay.

THE cock doth crow
To let you know,
If you be wise
'Tis time to rise.

I HAD two pigeons
  bright and gay,
They flew from me
  the other day;
What was the reason
  they did go?
I cannot tell, for I do
  not know.

Cock crows in the morn,
  To tell us to rise,
And he who lies late
  Will never be wise;

For early to bed,
  And early to rise,
Is the way to be healthy
  And wealthy and wise.

ROBIN-A-BOBBIN
  Bent his bow,

Shot at a pigeon,
  And killed a crow.

Pussy-cat ate the dumplings, the dumplings,
Pussy-cat ate the dumplings.
    Mamma stood by,
    And cried, Oh, fie!
Why did you eat the dumplings?

I had a little cow: to save her,
I turned her into the meadow to graze her;
There came a heavy storm of rain,
And drove the little cow home again.

The church doors they stood open,
And there the little cow was cropen;
The bell-ropes they were made of hay,
And the little cow ate them all away:
The sexton came to toll the bell,
And pushed the little cow into the well!

BETTY PRINGLE had a little pig,
Not very little and not very big.
When he was alive he lived in clover,
But now he's dead, and that's all over.
So Billy Pringle he laid down and cried,
And Betty Pringle she laid down and died;
So there was an end of one, two, and three:
  Billy Pringle he,
  Betty Pringle she,
  And the piggy wiggy.

 As I went to Bonner,
  I met a pig without a wig,
 Upon my word and honor.

THERE was a little one-eyed gunner,
Who killed all the birds that died last summer.

JACK SPRAT's pig,
He was not very little,
Nor yet very big;
He was not very lean,
He was not very fat;
He'll do well for a grunt,
Says little Jack Sprat.

A-MILKING, a milking, my maid:
"Cow, take care of your heels," she said:
"And you shall have some nice new hay
If you'll quietly let me milk away."

'T was once upon a time
  When Jenny Wren was young,
So daintily she danced,
  And so prettily she sung;
Robin Redbreast lost his heart,
  For he was a gallant bird;
So he doffed his hat to Jenny Wren,
  Requesting to be heard.

O dearest Jenny Wren,
  If you will but be mine,
You shall feed on cherry pie, you shall,
  And drink new currant wine;
I'll dress you like a goldfinch,
  Or any peacock gay;
So dearest Jen, if you'll be mine,
  Let us appoint the day.

Jenny blushed behind her fan,
  And thus declared her mind:
Since, dearest Bob, I love you well,
  I'll take your offer kind;
Cherry pie is very nice,
  And so is currant wine;
But I must wear my plain brown gown,
  And never go too fine.

Robin Redbreast rose up early,
  All at the break of day,
And he flew to Jenny Wren's house,
  And sung a roundelay;
He sung of Robin Redbreast
  And little Jenny Wren,
And when he came unto the end,
  He then began again.

CHARLEY WARLEY had a cow,
Black and white about the brow;
Open the gate and let her go through,
Charley Warley's old cow!

PUSSY-CAT MOLE
Jumped over a coal,
And in her best petticoat burnt a great hole.
Poor pussy's weeping,—she'll have no more milk
Until her best petticoat's mended with silk.

The following stanza is of very considerable antiquity, and is common in Yorkshire.—See Hunter's "Hallamshire Glossary," p. 56.

LADY-COW, lady-cow, fly thy way home,
Thy house is on fire, thy children all gone,
All but one, that ligs under a stone,
Fly thee home, lady-cow, ere it be gone.

ONCE I saw a little bird
Come hop, hop, hop;
So I cried, little bird,
Will you stop, stop, stop?
And was going to the window
To say, How do you do?
But he shook his little tail,
And far away he flew.

As titty mouse sat in the witty to spin,
Pussy came to her and bid her good ev'n.
"Oh, what are you doing, my little 'oman?"
"A-spinning a doublet for my gudeman."
"Then I shall come to thee, and wind up thy thread?"
"Oh, no, Mrs. Puss, you'll bite off my head."

THERE was a piper, he'd a cow,
  And he'd no hay to give her,
He took his pipes and played a tune.
  Consider, old cow, consider!

The cow considered very well,
  For she gave the piper a penny,
That he might play the tune again
  Of "Corn-rigs are bonnie!"

THERE was an old woman had three cows—
  Rosy and Colin and Dun:
Rosy and Colin were sold at the fair,
And Dun broke his head in a fit of despair;
And there was an end of her three cows—
  Rosy and Colin and Dun.

SHOE the colt,	Here a nail,
Shoe the colt;	There a nail,
Shoe the wild mare;	Yet she goes bare.

I HAD a little cow;
Hey-diddle, ho-diddle!
I had a little cow, and it had a little calf;
Hey-diddle, ho-diddle; and there's my song half.

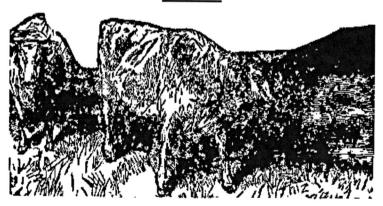

I had a little cow;
Hey-diddle, ho-diddle!
I had a little cow, and I drove it to the stall;
Hey-diddle, ho-diddle; and there's my song all!

LITTLE Jenny Wren fell sick upon a time;
In came Robin Redbreast, and brought her cake and wine.
Eat of my cake, Jenny, and drink of my wine.
Thank you, Robin, kindly, you shall be mine.

Jenny she got well, and stood upon her feet,
And told Robin plainly she loved him not a bit.
Robin he was angry, and hopped upon a twig,
Saying, Out upon you, fie upon you, bold-faced jig!

But Jenny Wren fell sick again, and Jenny Wren did die?
The doctors said they'd cure her, or know the reason why;
Doctor Hawk felt her pulse, and, shaking his head,
Said, I fear I can't save her, because she's quite dead!

Doctor Cat said—Indeed, I don't think she's dead;
I believe, if I try, she yet may be bled!—
You need not a lancet, Miss Pussy, indeed,
Your claws are enough a poor wren to bleed.

Why, Puss, you're quite foolish, exclaimed Doctor Goose;
To bleed a dead wren can be of no use!—
Ah, Doctor Goose, you're very wise;
Your learning profound might ganders surprise.

She'll do very well yet, exclaimed Doctor Fox,
If she'll take but two pills from out of this box!—
Ah, Doctor Fox, you are very cunning;
But if she's dead, you'll not get one in.

Doctor Jackass advanced—See this balsam: *I* make it!
She yet may survive, if you get her to take it!—
What you say, Doctor Ass, may be very true,
But I ne'er saw the dead drink—pray, doctor, did you?

Says Robin, Get out! you're a parcel of quacks;
Or I'll put this good stick about each of your backs.
So Robin began to bang them about;
They stayed for no fees, but were glad to get out.

> Cock Robin long for Jenny grieves,
> At last he covered her with leaves;
> And o'er the place a mournful lay
> For Jenny Wren sings every day.

THERE was a glossy blackbird once
  Lived in a cherry-tree,
He chirped and sung from morn till night,
  No bird so blithe as he?
And this the burden of his song
  Forever used to be:
Good boys shall have cherries as soon as they're ripe,
But naughty boys none from me.

> JOHNNY ARMSTRONG killed a calf;
> Peter Henderson got the half;
> Willy Wilkinson got the head,—
> Ring the bell, the calf is dead!

LITTLE Robin Redbreast With a pair of speckled legs,
  Sat upon a hurdle,   And a green girdle.

MARY had a pretty bird
  With feathers bright and
      yellow,
Slender legs — upon my
    word,
  He *was* a pretty fellow.

The sweetest notes he al-
    ways sang,
  Which much delighted
      Mary;
And near the cage she'd
    ever sit,
  To hear her own canary

SOME little mice sat in a barn to spin;
Pussy came by and popped her head in;
Shall I come in, and cut your threads off?
Oh no! kind sir, you will snap our heads off!"

FOUR-AND-TWENTY tailors went to kill a snail,
The best man among them durst not touch her tail;
She put out her horns like a little Kyloe cow,
Run, tailors, run! or she'll kill you all e'en now.

Bless you, bless you, bonny bee:
Say, when will your wedding be?
If it be to-morrow day,
Take your wings and fly away.

Dickery, dickery, dare,
The pig flew up in the
air;
The man in brown soon
brought him down,
Dickery, dickery, dare.

Gray goose and gander,
Waft your wings together,
And carry the good King's daughter
Over the one strand river.

Burnie bee, burnie bee,
Tell me when your wedding be?
If it be to-morrow day,
Take your wings and fly away.

Croak! said the Toad, I'm hungry, I think,
To-day I've had nothing to eat or to drink,
I'll crawl to a garden and jump through the pales,
And there I'll dine nicely on slugs and on snails;
Ho, ho! quoth the frog, is that what you mean?
Then I'll hop away to the next meadow stream,
There I will drink, and eat worms and slugs too,
And then I shall have a good dinner like you.

Hie, hie, says Anthony,
Puss in the pantry
Gnawing, gnawing,
A mutton, mutton-bone;
See how she tumbles it,
See now she mumbles it,
See how she tosses
The mutton, mutton-bone.

Who killed Cock Robin ?
  I, said the Sparrow,
  With my bow and arrow.

Who saw him die ?
  I, said the Fly,
  With my little eye.

Who caught his blood ?
  I, said the Fish,
  With my little dish.

Who'll make his shroud?
I, said the Beetle,
With my thread aud
needle.

Who'll dig his grave?
I, said the Owl,
With my spade and
shovel.

Who'll carry him to the
grave?
I, said the Kite,
If it's not in the night.

Who'll carry the link?
I, said the Linnet,
I'll fetch it in a minute.

Who'll be chief mourner?
I, said the Dove,
For I mourn for my
love.

Who'll sing a psaim?
I, said the Thrush,
As he sat in a bush.

Who'll be the parson?
I, said the Rook,
With my little book.

Who'll be the clerk?
I, said the Lark,
If it's not in the dark.

Who'll toll the bell?
I, said the Bull,
Because I can pull.

All the birds of the air
  Fell a-sighing and sob-
      bing,

When they heard the bell
      toll
  For poor Cock Robin.

"ROBERT Barnes, fellow fine,
　　Can you shoe this horse of mine?"
"Yes, good sir, that I can,
　　As well as any other man:
　　There's a nail, and there's a prod,
　　And now, good sir, your horse is shod."

———

I HAD a little dog, and they called
　　him Buff;
I sent him to the shop for a hap'-
　　orth of snuff;
But he lost the bag, and spilt the
　　snuff,
So take that cuff, and that's
　　enough.

———

As I went over the water,
The water went over me,
I saw two little blackbirds sitting on a tree:
The one called me a rascal,
The other called me a thief;
I took up my little black stick,
And knocked out all their teeth.

———

THE winds they did blow,
　　The leaves they did wag;
Along came a beggar boy,
　　And put me in his bag.

He took me up to London,
　　A lady did me buy,
Put me in a silver cage,
　　And hung me up on high.

With apples by the fire,
　　And nuts for to crack,
Besides a little feather bed
　　To rest my little back.

THREE little kittens they lost their mittens,
  And they began to cry,
"Oh! mammy dear,
We sadly fear,
  Our mittens we have lost!"
"What! lost your mittens,
You naughty kittens,
  Then you shall have no pie."
    Miew, miew, miew, miew,
    Miew, miew, miew, miew.

The three little kittens they found their mittens,
  And they began to cry,
"Oh! mammy dear,
See here, see here,
  Our mittens we have found."

"What! found your mittens,
You little kittens,
   Then you shall have some pie."
     Purr, purr, purr, purr,
     Purr, purr, purr, purr.

The three little kittens put on their mittens,
   And soon ate up the pie;
"Oh! mammy dear,
We greatly fear,
   Our mittens we have soil'd."
"What! soil'd your mittens,
You naughty kittens!"
   Then they began to sigh,
     Miew, miew, miew, miew,
     Miew, miew, miew, miew.

The three little kittens they washed their mittens.
    And hung them up to dry;
"Oh! mammy dear,
Look here, look here,
    Our mittens we have wash'd.
"What! wash'd your mittens,
You darling kittens!
    But I smell a rat close by!
Hush! hush!" Miew, miew,
Miew, miew, miew, miew.

A FARMER went trotting
    Upon his grey mare,
Bumpety, bumpety,
        bump!
With his daughter be-
        hind him,
So rosy and fair,
    Lumpety, lumpety,
        lump!

A raven cried Croak!
　And they all tumbled down,
Bumpety, bumpety, bump!
　The mare broke her knees,
And the farmer his crown,
　Lumpety, lumpety, lump!

The mischievous raven
　Flew laughing away,
Bumpety, bumpety, bump!
　And vowed he would serve them
The same the next day,
　Lumpety, lumpety, lump!

———

Pussy sat by the fireside
In a basket full of coal-dust;
Bas-
ket,
Coal-
dust,
In a basket full of coal-dust!

FIFTEENTH CLASS.

Relics.

THE girl in the lane, that couldn't speak plain,
　Cried "Gobble, gobble, gobble:"
The man on the hill, that couldn't stand still,
　Went hobble, hobble, hobble.

BABY and I
Were baked in a pie,
The gravy was wonderful
　hot:

We had nothing to pay
　To the baker that day
And so we crept out of the
　pot.

WHAT's the news of the day,
Good neighbor, I pray?

They say the balloon
Is gone up to the moon!

GIRLS and boys, come out to play,
The moon doth shine as bright as day;
Leave your supper and leave your sleep,
And come with your playfellows into the street.
Come with a whoop, come with a call,
Come with a good will or not at all.
Up the ladder and down the wall,
A halfpenny roll will serve us all.
You find milk, and I'll find flour,
And we'll have a pudding in half an hour.

WILLY boy, Willy boy, where are you going?
  I will go with you, if that I may.
I'm going to the meadow to see them a-mowing,
  I'm going to help them to make the hay.

HINK, minx! the old witch winks,
　The fat begins to fry:
There's nobody at home but jumping Joan,
　Father, mother, and I.

HARK, hark!　　　　Some in jags,
The dogs do bark,　　Some in rags,
Beggars are coming to　And some in velvet gowns.
　town;

SHAKE a leg, wag a leg, when will you gang?
At midsummer, mother, when the days are lang.

CHARLEY wag,
  Ate the pudding and left the bag.

WE'RE all in the dumps,
  For diamonds are trumps;
The kittens are gone to St. Paul's!
  The babies are bit,
  The moon's in a fit,
And the houses are built without walls

  I HAD a little moppet,
  I put it in my pocket,
And fed it with corn and hay:
  Then came a proud beggar,
  And swore he would have her,
And stole little moppet away.

To market, to market, a gallop, a trot,
To buy some meat to put in the pot;
Threepence a quarter, a groat a side,
If it hadn't been killed, it must have died.

THE children of Holland
   Take pleasure in making
What the children of England
   Take pleasure in breaking.*

* Alluding to toys, a great number of which are imported from Holland.

THE barber shaveᴅ the mason, As I suppose Cut off his nose, And popped it in a basin.

COME, let's to bed,
Says Sleepy-head;
  Tarry awhile, says
    Slow;
Put on the pot,
Says Greedy-gut,
  Let's sup before we
    go.

LITTLE girl, little girl, where have you been ?
Gathering roses to give to the Queen.
Little girl, little girl, what gave she you ?
She gave me a diamond as big as my shoe.

BARBER, barber, shave a pig,
How many hairs will make a wig?
" Four-and-twenty, that's enough."
Give the barber a pinch of snuff.

IF all the seas were one sea,
What a *great* sea that would be!
And if all the trees were one tree,
What a *great* tree that would be!
And if all the axes were one axe,
What a *great* axe that would be!
And if all the men were one man,
What a *great* man he would be!
And if the *great* man took the *great* axe,
And cut down the *great* tree,
And let it fall into the *great* sea,
What a splish-splash *that* would be!

RAIN, rain, go away,   Little   Arthur   wants   to
Come again another day;   play.

HANNAH BANTRY in the pantry,
   Eating a mutton-bone;
How she gnawed it, how she clawed it,
   When she found she was alone !

DARBY and Joan were dressed in black,
Sword and buckle behind their back;
Foot for foot, and knee for knee,
Turn about Darby's company.

WHAT are little boys made of, made of?
What are little boys made of?
Snaps and snails, and puppy-dogs' tails;
And that's what little boys are made of, made of.
What are little girls made of, made of, made of?
What are little girls made of?
Sugar and spice, and all that's nice;
And that's what little girls are made of, made of.

DAYS OF BIRTH.

MONDAY'S child is fair in face,
Tuesday's child is full of grace,
Wednesday's child is full of woe,
Thursday's child has far to go,
Friday's child is loving and giving,
Saturday's child works hard for its living;
And a child that's born on Christmas day
Is fair and wise, good and gay.

FINGER-NAILS.

There is a superstition, says Forby, ii., 411, respecting cutting the nails, and some days are considered more lucky for this operation than others. To cut them on a Tuesday is thought particularly auspicious. Indeed, if we are to believe an old rhyming saw on this subject, every day of the week is endowed with its several and peculiar virtue, if the nails are invariably cut on that day and no other. The lines are as follows:

Cut them on Monday, you cut them for health;

Cut them on Tuesday, you cut them for wealth;

Cut them on Wednesday, you cut them for news;

Cut them on Thursday, a new pair of shoes;

Cut them on Friday, you cut them for sorrow;

Cut them on Saturday, see your true love to-morrow;

Cut them on Sunday, ill luck will be with you all the week.

———

The following divination rhymes refer to the *gifts*, or white spots on the nails, beginning with the thumb, and going on regularly to the little finger. The last gift will show the destiny of the operator *pro tempore.*

A GIFT—a friend—a foe—
A journey—to go.

———

COLORS.

Color superstitions, though rapidly disappearing, still obtain in the remote rural districts. The following lines were obtained from the east of England:

BLUE is true,   Red's brazen,
Yellow's jealous,   White is love,
Green's forsaken,   And black is death.

———

Go to bed, Tom!
Go to bed, Tom!
Drunk or sober,
Go to bed, Tom.

Who comes here ?—A grenadier.
What do you want ?—A pot of beer.
Where is your money ?—I've forgot.
Get you gone, you drunken sot!

The quaker's wife got up to bake,
  Her children all about her,
She gave them every one a cake,
  And the miller wants his moulter.

As I went over the water,
  The water went over me,
I heard an old woman cry-
    ing,
  Will you buy some fur-
    mity?

HIGH diddle doubt, my
  candle out,
  My little maid is not at
  home:
Saddle my hog, and bridle
  my dog,
  And fetch my little maid
  home.

LITTLE Mary Ester,
  Sat upon a tester,
Eating of curds and whey;
  There came a little spider,
  And set him down beside her,
And frightened Mary Ester away.

LITTLE Tommy Tacket,
  Sits upon his cracket;
Half a yard of cloth will make him coat and jacket,
  Make him coat and jacket,
  Trowsers to the knee.
And if you will not have him, you may let him be.

PEG, Peg, with a wooden leg,
  Her father was a miller:
He tossed the dumpling at her head,
  And said he could not kill her.

WHEN Jacky's a very good boy,
  He shall have cakes and a custard;
But when he does nothing but cry,
  He shall have nothing but mustard.

Little Tom Tucker
Sings for his supper;
What shall he eat?
White bread and butter.

How shall he cut it
Without e'er a knife?
How will he be married
Without e'er a wife?

LITTLE Miss Muffet,
She sat on a tuffet,
Eating of curds and whey;
There came a great spi-
der,
Who sat down beside
her,
And frightened Miss Muf-
fet away.

LITTLE Miss, pretty Miss, If I had half-a-crown a day,
Blessings light upon you; I'd spend it all upon you.

MY little old man and I fell out,
I'll tell you what 'twas all about:
I had money, and he had none,
And that's the way the row begun.

BLOW, wind, blow! and go, mill,
    go!
That the miller may grind his
    corn;
That the baker may take it,
And into rolls make it,
And send us some hot in the
    morn.

Wash, hands, wash,
  Daddy's gone to plough,
If you want your hands washed
Have them washed now.

A formula for making young children submit to the operation of having their hands washed. *Mutatis mutandis*, the lines will serve as a specific for everything of the kind, as brushing hair, &c.

Parson Darby wore a black gown,
And every button cost half-a-crown;
From port to port, and toe to toe,
Turn the ship, and away we go!

Daffy-down-dilly has come up to town,
In a yellow petticoat and a green gown.

The following is quoted in the song of Mad Tom. See Halliwell's introduction to Shakespeare's "Midsummer Night's Dream," p. 55.

The man in the moon drinks claret,
  But he is a dull Jack-a-Dandy;
Would he know a sheep's head from a carrot
  He should learn to drink cider and brandy.

A good child, a good child,   At the tickling of your
   As I suppose you be,   knee.
Never laughed nor smiled

How many days has my baby to play?
   Saturday, Sunday, Monday,
Tuesday, Wednesday, Thursday, Friday,
   Saturday, Sunday, Monday.

   Blenky my nutty-cock,
     Blenk him away;
   My nutty-cock's never
     Been blenked to-day.
What wi' carding and spinning on t' wheel,
We've never had time to blenk nutty-cock weel;
But let to-morrow come ever so sune,
My nutty-cock it sall be blenked by nune.

Around the green gravel the grass grows green.
And all the pretty maids were plain to be seen;
Wash them with milk, and clothe them with silk,
And write their names with a pen and ink.

To market, to market, to buy a plum cake,
Back again, back again, baby is late;
To market, to market, to buy a plum bun,
Back again, back again, market is done.

As I was going to sell my eggs,
I met a man with bandy legs,
Bandy legs and crooked toes,—
I tripped up his heels, and he fell on his nose.

How do you do, neighbor?
Neighbor, how do you do?—
  I am pretty well,
And how does Cousin Sue do?—
  She's pretty well,
And sends her duty to you;
  So does bonnie Nell—
Good lack! how does she do?

Sᴛ. Tʜᴏᴍᴀs's Dᴀʏ is past and gone,
And Christmas is a'most a-come.
Maidens, arise
And make your pies,
And save poor Tailor Bobby some.

Oʟᴅ Sir Simon the King,
And young Sir Simon the 'squire,
And old Mrs. Hickabout
Kicked Mrs. Kickabout
Round about our coal fire!

SIXTEENTH CLASS.

Local.

THERE was a little nobby colt,
  His name was Nobby Gray;
His head was made of pouce straw,
  His tail was made of hay.
He could ramble, he could trot,
He could carry a mustard-pot
Round the town of Woodstock.
  Hey, Jenny, hey!

KING's Sutton is a pretty town,
  And lies all in a valley;
There is a pretty ring of bells,
  Besides a bowling-alley;
Wine and liquor in good store,
  Pretty maidens plenty:
Can a man desire more?
  There ain't such a town in
    twenty.

THE little priest of Felton,
The little priest of Felton,
He killed a mouse within his house,
And ne'er a one to help him!!

THE following verses are said by Aubrey to have been sung in his time by the girls of Oxfordshire in a sport called "Leap Candle," which is now obsolete. See Thoms' "Anecdotes and Traditions," p. 96.

THE tailor of Bicester,
He has but one eye;
He cannot cut a pair of green galagaskins
If he were to try.

DICK and Tom, Will and John,
Brought me from Nottingham.

AT Brill-on-the-Hill
The wind blows shrill,
The cook no meat can dress;
At Stow-in-the-Wold
The wind blows cold,—
I know no more than this.

A LITTLE bit of powdered beef,
And a great net of cabbage,
The best meal I have had to-day
Is a good bowl of porridge.

MY father and mother, my uncle and aunt,
Be all gone to Norton, but little Jack and I.

LITTLE boy, pretty boy, where were you born?
In Lincolnshire, master: come, blow the cow's horn.
A halfpennny pudding, a penny pie,
A shoulder of mutton, and that love I.

A MAN went a-hunting at Reigate,
And wished to leap over a high gate;
  Says the owner, "Go round,
  With your gun and your hound,
For you never shall leap over my gate."

DRIDDLETY drum, driddlety drum,
There you see the beggars are come;
Some are here, and some are there,
And some are gone to Chidley Fair.

LITTLE lad, little lad, where
    wast thou born ?
Far off in Lancashire, under a
    thorn,
Where they sop sour milk in a
    ram's horn.

LINCOLN was, and London is,
    And York shall be
    The fairest city of the three.

ISLE OF MAN.

ALL the bairns unborn will rue the day
That the Isle of Man was sold away;
And there's ne'er a wife that loves a dram,
But what will lament for the Isle of Man.

I LOST my mare in Lincoln Lane,
   And couldn't tell where to find her,
Till she came home both lame and blind,
   With never a tail behind her.

CRIPPLE Dick upon a stick,   Riding away to Galloway,
  And Sandy on a sow,   To buy a pound o' woo.

SEVENTEENTH CLASS.
Love and Matrimony.

As I was going up Pippen Hill,
  Pippen Hill was dirty,
There I met a pretty miss,
  And she dropt me a curtsey.

Little miss, pretty miss,
  Blessings light upon you:
If I had half-a-crown a day,
  I'd spend it all upon you.

It's once I courted as pretty a lass
  As ever your eyes did see;
But now she's come to such a pass,
  She never will do for me.

She invited me to her own house,
  Where oft I'd been before,
And she tumbled me into the hog-tub,
  And I'll never go there any more.

BRAVE news is come to town,
Brave news is carried;

Brave news is come to town,—
Jemmy Dawson's married.

As Tommy Snooks and Bessy Brooks
Were walking out one Sunday,
Says Tommy Snooks to Bessy Brooks,
"To-morrow will be Monday."

WHAT care I how black I be?
Twenty pounds will marry me;
If twenty won't, forty shall,—
I am my mother's bouncing girl!

WILLY, Willy Wilkin,
Kissed the maids a-milk-
ing,
    Fa, la, la!

And with his merry daffing
He set them all a-laugh-
ing,
    Ha, ha, ha!

I LOVE my love with an A because he's Agreeable.
I hate him because he's Avaricious.
He took me to the sign of the Acorn,
And treated me with Apples.
His name's Andrew,
And he lives at Arlington.

SYLVIA, sweet as morning air,
Do not drive me to despair:
Long have I sighed in vain,
Now I am come again,
　　Will you be mine or no, no-a-no,—
　　Will you be mine or no?

Simon, pray leave off your suit,
For of your courting you'll reap no fruit;
I would rather give a crown
Than be married to a clown;
   Go for a booby, go, no-a-no,—
   Go for a booby, go.

" WHERE have you been all the day,
    My boy Willy?"
" I've been all the day
  Courting of a lady gay:
  But oh! she's too young
  To be taken from her mammy."
" What work can she do,
    My boy Willy?
  Can she bake and can she brew,
    My boy Willy?"
" She can brew and she can bake,
  And she can make our wedding cake:
  But oh! she's too young
  To be taken from her mammy."
" What age may she be? What age may she be,
    My boy Willy?"
" Twice two, twice seven,
  Twice ten, twice eleven:
  But oh! she's too young
  To be taken from her mammy."

    A cow and a calf,
    An ox and a half,
  Forty good shillings and three;
    Is that not enough tocher
    For a shoemaker's daughter,
  A bonny lass with a black e'e?

This is part of a little work called "Authentic Memoirs of the little Man and the little Maid, with some interesting particulars of their lives," which I suspect is more modern than the following. Walpole printed a small broadside containing a different version.

THERE was a little man,
And he woo'd a little maid,
And he said, "Little maid, will you wed, wed, wed?
I have little more to say
Than will you, yea or nay?
For least said is soonest men-ded, ded, ded."

The little maid replied,
(Some say a little sighed,)
" But what shall we have for to eat, eat, eat?
Will the love that you're so rich in
Make a fire in the kitchen?
Or the little God of Love turn the spit, spit, spit?"

LITTLE Jack Jingle,
He used to live single;
But when he got tired of this kind of life,
He left off being single, and lived with his wife.

WHEN shall we be married,
  My dear Nicholas Wood?
We will be married on Monday,
  And will not that be very good?
What, shall we be married no sooner?
  Why, sure the man's gone wood!*

What shall we have for our dinner,
  My dear Nicholas Wood?
We will have bacon and pudding,
  And will not that be very good?
What, shall we have nothing more?
  Why, sure the man's gone wood!

Who shall we have at our wedding,
  My dear Nicholas Wood?
We will have mammy and daddy,
  And will not that be very good?
What, shall we have nobody else?
  Why, sure the man's gone wood.

* Mad. This sense of the word has long been obsolete; and exhibits, therefore, the antiquity of these lines.

O THE little rusty, dusty, rusty miller!
I'll not change my wife for either gold or siller.

I AM a pretty girl,
  As fair as any pearl,
And sweethearts I can get none;
  But every girl that's plain
  Can many sweethearts gain,
And I, pretty girl, can't get one.

Up hill and down dale;
Butter is made in every vale
And if that Nancy Cook
Is a good girl,
She shall have a spouse,
And make butter anon,
Before her old grandmother
Grows a young man.

We're all dry with drinking on 't,
We're all dry with drinking on 't;
The piper spoke to the fiddler's
  wife,
And I can't sleep for thinking
  on 't.

Rosemary green,
  And lavender blue,
Thyme and sweet marjoram,
  Hyssop and rue.

Did you see my wife, did you see, did you see,
  Did you see my wife looking for me?
She wears a straw bonnet with white ribbon on it,
  And dimity petticoats over her knee.

The practice of sowing hemp-seed on Allhallows Even is often alluded to by earlier writers, and Gay, in his "Pastorals," quotes part of the following lines as used on that occasion:

Hemp-seed I set,
  Hemp-seed I sow,

The young man that I love,
  Come after me and mow!

On Saturday night
Shall be all my care
To powder my locks
And curl my hair.

On Sunday morning
My love will come in,
When he will marry me.
With a gold ring.

Tommy Trot, a man of law,
Sold his bed and lay upon straw,—
Sold the straw and slept on grass,
To buy his wife a looking-glass.

———

Where have you been to-day, Billy, my son?
Where have you been to-day, my only man?
I've been a-wooing, mother; make my bed soon,
For I'm sick at heart, and fain would lie down.

What have you ate to-day, Billy, my son?
What have you ate to-day, my only man?
I've ate an eel pie, mother; make my bed soon,
For I am sick at heart, and shall die before noon!

" LITTLE maid, pretty maid, whither
    goest thou?"
" Down in the forest to milk my cow."
" Shall I go with thee?" " No, not
    now;
    When I send for thee, then come
    thou."

BIRDS of a feather flock together,
    And so will pigs and swine;
Rats and mice will have their choice,
    And so will I have mine.

LITTLE Jack Dandy-prat was my first suitor;
He had a dish and a spoon, and he'd some pewter;
He'd linen and woollen, and woollen and linen,
A little pig in a string cost him five shilling.

JACK SPRAT could eat no fat,
  His wife could eat no lean;
And so, betwixt them both, you see,
  They licked the platter clean.

He. IF you with me will go, my love,
    You shall see a pretty show, my love,
      Let dame say what she will:
    If you will have me, my love,
     I will have thee, my love,
        So let the milk-pail stand still.

She. Since you have said so, my love,
    Longer I will go, my love,
      Let dame say what she will:
    If you will have me, my love,
    I will have thee, my love,
        So let the milk-pail stand still.

  JACK in the pulpit, out and in,
  Sold his wife for a minikin pin,

THE KEYS OF CANTERBURY.

OH, madam, I will give you the keys of Canterbury,
To set all the bells ringing when we shall be merry;
If you will but walk abroad with me,
If you will but talk with me.

Sir, I'll not accept of the keys of Canterbury,
To set all the bells ringing when we shall be merry;
Neither will I walk abroad with thee,
Neither will I talk with thee!

Oh, madam, I will give you a fine carved comb,
To comb out your ringlets when I am from home,
If you will but walk with me, &c.
Sir, I'll not accept, &c.

Oh, madam, I will give you a pair of shoes of cork,*
One made in London, the other made in York,
If you will but walk with me, &c.
Sir, I'll not accept, &c.

Madam, I will give you a sweet silver bell,†
To ring up your maidens when you are not well,
If you will but walk with me, &c.
Sir, I'll not accept, &c.

Oh, my man John, what can the matter be ?
I love the lady and the lady loves not me!
Neither will she walk abroad with me,
Neither will she talk with me

Oh, master dear, do not despair,
The lady she shall be, shall be your only dear,
And she will walk and talk with thee,
And she will walk with thee!

* This proves the song was not later than the era of chopines, or high cork shoes.

† Another proof of antiquity. It must probably have been written before the invention of bell-pulls.

Oh, madam, I will give you the keys of my chest,
To count my gold and silver when I am gone to rest,
If you will but walk abroad with me,
If you will but talk with me.

Oh, sir, I will accept of the keys of your chest,
To count your gold and silver when you are gone to rest,
And I will walk abroad with thee,
And I will talk with thee!

Oh! mother, I shall be married to Mr. Punchinello.
          To Mr. Punch,
          To Mr. Chin,
          To Mr. Nell,
          To Mr. Lo,
          Mr. Punch, Mr. Chin,
          Mr. Nell, Mr. Lo,
          To Mr. Punchinello.

"Madam, I am come to court you
  If your favor I can gain."
"Ah, ah!" said she, "you are a bold fellow,
  If I e'er see your face again!"
" Madam, I have rings and diamonds,
  Madam, I have houses and land,
  Madam, I have a world of treasure,—
  All shall be at your command."
" I care not for rings and diamonds,
  I care not for houses and land,
  I care not for a world of treasure,
  So that I have but a handsome man."
"Madam, you think much of beauty:
  Beauty hasteneth to decay,
  For the fairest of flowers that grow in summer
  Will decay and fade away."

CAN you make me a cambric shirt,
　Parsley, sage, rosemary, and thyme,
Without any seam or needlework?
　And you shall be a true lover of mine.

Can you wash it in yonder well,
　Parsley, &c.
Where never sprung water, nor rain ever fell?
　And you, &c.

Can you dry it on yonder thorn,
　Parsley, &c.
Which never bore blossom since Adam was born?
　And you, &c.

Now you have asked me questions three,
　Parsley, &c.
I hope you'll answer as many for me,
　And you, &c.

Can you find me an acre of land,
　Parsley, &c.
Between the salt water and the sea-sand?
　And you, &c.

Can you plough it with a ram's horn,
　Parsley, &c.,
And sow it all over with one peppercorn?
　And you, &c.

Can you reap it with a sickle of leather,
　Parsley, &c.
And bind it up with a peacock's feather?
　And you, &c.

When you have done and finished your work,
　Parsley, &c.
Then come to me for your cambric shirt,
　And you, &c.

I DOUBT, I doubt my fire is out,
  My little wife isn't at home;
I'll saddle my dog, and I'll bridle my cat,
  And I'll go fetch my little wife home.

MADAM, I will give you a fine silken gown,
Nine yards wide and eleven yards long,
  If you will be my gay ladye.

Sir, I won't accept your fine silken gown,
Nine yards wide and eleven yards long,
  Nor will I be your gay ladye.

John, my man, how can this matter be?
I love a lady who doesn't love me,
  Nor will she be my gay ladye.

Peace, master, peace; you need not fear,
She'll be your love and only dear,
  But the gold ring only will gain you her.

Madam, I'll give you a fine golden ring,
To go to church to be married in,
  If you will be my gay ladye.

Sir, I will accept your fine golden ring,
To go to church to be married in,
  And I will be your gay ladye.

John, my man, here's a crown for thee,
For winning me this gay ladye.

This nursery song may probably commemorate a part of Tom Thumb's history, extant in a little Danish work, treating of " Swain Tomling, a man no bigger than a thumb, who would be married to a woman three ells and three quarters long."   See Mr. Thoms' Preface to " Tom à Lincoln," p. xi.

I HAD a little husband
　　No bigger than my thumb,
I put him in a pint pot,
　　And there I bid him drum.

I bought a little horse,
   That galloped up and down;
I bridled him, and saddled him,
   And sent him out of town.

I gave him some garters,
   To garter up his hose,
And a little handkerchief,
   To wipe his pretty nose.

———

THOMAS and Annis met in the dark.
  "Good morning," said Thomas.
  "Good morning," said Annis.
And so they began to talk.

  " I'll give you," says Thomas—
  "Give me," says Annis;
    "I prithee, love, tell me what?"
  "Some nuts," said Thomas.
  "Some nuts?" said Annis;
    "Nuts are good to crack."

  "I love you," said Thomas.
  "Love me!" said Annis;
    "I prithee, love, tell me where?"
  "In my heart," said Thomas.
  "In your heart!" said Annis;
    "How came you to love me there?"

  "I'll marry you," said Thomas.
  "Marry me!" said Annis;
    "I prithee, love, tell me when?"
    "Next Sunday," said Thomas.
  "Next Sunday!" said Annis;
    "I wish next Sunday were come."

Young Roger came tapping at Dolly's window,
    Thumpaty, thumpaty, thump!
He asked for admittance; she answered him "No!"
    Frumpaty, frumpaty, frump!
"No, no, Roger, no! as you came you may go!"
    Stumpaty, stumpaty, stump!

I MARRIED my wife by the light of the moon,
  A tidy housewife, a tidy one;
She never gets up until it is noon,
  And I hope she'll prove a tidy one.

And when she gets up, she is slovenly laced,
  A tidy, &c.
She takes up the poker to roll out the paste,
  And I hope, &c.

She churns her butter in a boot,
  A tidy, &c.
And instead of a churn-staff she puts in her foot,
  And I hope, &c.

She lays her cheese on the scullery shelf,
  A tidy, &c.
And she never turns it till it turns itself,
  And I hope, &c.

———

MASTER I have, and I am his man,
  Gallop a dreary dun;
Master I have, and I am his man,
And I'll get a wife as fast as I can;
With a heighly gaily gamberally,
  Higgledy piggledy, niggledy, niggledy,
  Gallop a dreary dun.

———

SAW ye aught of my love a-coming from the market?
  A peck of meal upon her back,
  A babby in her basket;
Saw ye aught of my love a-coming from the market?

———

UP street, and down street,
  Each window's made of glass;
If you go to Tommy Tickler's house,
  You'll find a pretty lass.

PETER, Peter, pumpkin eater,
Had a wife and couldn't keep her—
He put her in a pumpkin shell,
And there he kept her very well.

———

BESSY BELL and Mary Gray,
  They were two bonny lasses:
They built their house upon the lea,
  And covered it with rashes.

Bessy kept the garden gate,
  And Mary kept the pantry;
Bessy always had to wait,
  While Mary lived in plenty.

———

CURLY locks! curly locks! wilt thou be mine?
Thou shalt not wash dishes, nor yet feed the swine;
But sit on a cushion and sew a fine seam,
And feed upon strawberries, sugar, and cream.

Cumberland Courtship.

BONNY lass, canny lass, willta be mine?
Thou'se neither wesh dishes, nor sarrah (*serve*) the
    swine;
Thou sall sit on a cushion, and sew up a seam,
And thou sall eat strawberries, sugar, and cream.

MARGARET wrote a letter,
Sealed it with her finger,
Threw it in the dam
For the dusty miller.
Dusty was his coat,
Dusty was the siller,
Dusty was the kiss
I'd from the dusty miller,
If I had my pockets
Full of gold and siller,
I would give it all
To my dusty miller.

Chorus.   Oh, the little, little
Rusty, dusty miller.

HERE comes a lusty woer,
  My a dildin, my a dal-
    din;
Here comes a lusty woer,
  Lily bright and shine a'.

For your fairest daughter,
  My a dildin, my a dal-
    din,
For your fairest daughter,
  Lily bright and shine a'.

Pray who do you woo,
  My a dildin, my a dal-
    din?
Pray, who do you woo,
  Lily bright and shine a'?

Then there she is for you,
  My a dildin, my a dal-
    din;
Then there she is for you,
  Lily bright and shine a'.

BLUE eye beauty,
Grey eye greedy,

Black eye blackie,
Brown eye brownie.

JACK and Jill went up the hill,
  To fetch a pail of water;

Jack fell down and broke his crown,
And Jill came tumbling after.

Little Jane ran up the lane,
 To hang her clothes a-drying
She called for Nell to ring the bell,
 For Jack and Jill were dying.

Nimble Dick ran up so quick,
 He tumbled over a timber,
And bent his bow to shoot a crow,
 And killed a cat in the window.

LITTLE Tom Dandy
 Was my first suitor,
He had a spoon and dish,
 And a little pewter.

O RARE Harry Parry,
 When will you marry?
When apples and pears are ripe,
 I'll come to your wedding,
 Without any bidding,
And dance and sing all the night.

Rowley Powley, pudding and
    pie,
Kissed the girls and made them
    cry;
When the girls begin to cry,
Rowley Powley runs away.

Love your own, kiss your own,
    Love your own mother, hinny,
For if she was dead and gone,
    You'd ne'er get such another,
      hinny.

There was a little pretty lad,
  And he lived by himself,
And all the meat he got
  He put upon a shelf.

The rats and the mice
  Did lead him such a life,
That he went to Ireland
  To get himself a wife.

The lanes they were so broad,
  And the fields they were so narrow,
He couldn't get his wife home
  Without a wheelbarrow.

The wheelbarrow broke,
  My wife she got a kick,
The deuce take the wheelbarrow,
  That spared my wife's neck.

LITTLE Johnny Jiggy Jag,
He rode a penny nag,
   And went to Wigan to woo:
When he came to a beck,
He fell and broke his neck,—
   Johnny, how dost thou now?

I made him a hat,
Of my coat-lap,
   And stockings of pearly
     blue:
A hat and a feather,
To keep out cold weather;
   So, Johnny, how dost
     thou now?

EIGHTEENTH CLASS.

Accumulative Stories.

JOHN BALL shot them all;
John Scott made the shot,
　But John Ball shot them all.
John Wyming made the priming,
And John Brammer made the rammer,
And John Scott made the shot,
　But John Ball shot them all.

John Block made the stock,
　And John Brammer made the rammer,
And John Wyming made the priming.
And John Scott made the shot,
　But John Ball shot them all.

John Crowder made the powder,
And John Block made the stock,
And John Wyming made the priming,
And John Brammer made the rammer,
And John Scott made the shot,
  But John Ball shot them all.

John Puzzle made the muzzle,
And John Crowder made the powder,
And John Block made the stock,
And John Wyming made the priming,
And John Brammer made the rammer,
And John Scott made the shot,
  But John Ball shot them all.

John Clint made the flint,
And John Puzzle made the muzzle,
And John Crowder made the powder,
And John Block made the stock,
And John Wyming made the priming,
And John Brammer made the rammer,
And John Scott made the shot,
  But John Ball shot them all.

John Patch made the match,
John Clint made the flint,
John Puzzle made the muzzle,
John Crowder made the powder,
John Block made the stock,
John Wyming made the priming,
John Brammer made the rammer,
John Scott made the shot,
  But John Ball shot them all.

THIS is the House that Jack built

THIS is the MALT
That lay in the House that Jack built.

THIS is the RAT
That ate the Malt,
That lay in the House that Jack built.

THIS is the CAT
That killed the Rat,
That ate the Malt,
That lay in the House that Jack built.

THIS is the DOG
That worried the Cat,
That killed the Rat,
That ate the Malt,
That lay in the House that Jack built.

HIS is the COW with the crumpled horn
That tossed the Dog,
That worried the Cat,
That killed the Rat,
That ate the Malt.
That lay in the House that Jack built.

HIS is the MAIDEN all forlorn,
That milked the Cow with the crumpled horn.
That tossed the Dog,
That worried the Cat,
That killed the Rat,
That ate the Malt,
That lay in the House that Jack built.

HIS is the MAN all tattered and torn

That kissed the Maiden all forlorn

That milked the Cow

with the crumpled horn

That tossed the Dog,

That worried the Cat,

That killed the Rat,

That ate the Malt,

That lay in the House

that Jack built.

THIS is the PRIEST all shaven and shorn,

That married the Man all tattered and torn,

That kissed the Maiden all forlorn,

That milked the Cow with the crumpled horn,

That tossed the Dog,

That worried the Cat,

That killed the Rat,

That ate the Malt,

That lay in the House that Jack built.

THIS is the COCK that crowed in the morn,
That waked the Priest all shaven and shorn,
That married the Man all tattered and torn,
That kissed the Maiden all forlorn,
That milked the cow with the crumpled horn,
That tossed the Dog,
That worried the Cat,
That killed the Rat,
That ate the Malt,
That lay in the House that Jack built.

THIS is the FARMER who sowed the corn,

That fed the Cock that crowed in the morn,

That waked the Priest all shaven and shorn,

That married the Man all tattered and torn,

That kissed the Maiden all forlorn,

That milked the Cow with the crumpled horn,

That tossed the Dog,

That worried the Cat,

That killed the Rat,

That ate the Malt,

That lay in the House that Jack built.

THIS is the HORSE and the HOUND and the HORN

That belonged to the Farmer who sowed the corn,

That fed the Cock that crowed in the morn,

That waked the Priest all shaven and shorn,

That married the Man all tattered and torn,

That kissed the Maiden all forlorn,

That milked the Cow with the crumpled horn,

That tossed the Dog,

That worried the Cat,

That killed the Rat,

That ate the Malt,

That lay in the House that Jack built.

The original of "The house that Jack built" is presumed to be a hymn in "*Seper Haggadah*," fol. 23, a translation of which is here given. The historical interpretation was first given by P. N. Leberecht, at Leipsic, in 1731, and is printed in the "Christian Reformer," vol. xvii., p. 28. The original is in the Chaldee language, and it may be mentioned that a very fine Hebrew manuscript of the fable, with illuminations, is in the possession of George Offer, Esq., London. It is inserted in the Hebrew Passover Service Book and concludes the service for the first two nights of the Passover.

1. A *kid, a kid*, my father bought
   For two pieces of money:

   > A kid, a kid.

2. Then came *the cat*, and ate the kid,
   That my father bought
   For two pieces of money:

   > A kid, a kid.

3. Then came *the dog*, and bit the cat,
   That ate the kid,
   That my father bought
   For two pieces of money:

   > A kid, a kid.

4. Then came *the staff*, and beat the dog,
   That bit the cat,
   That ate the kid,
   That my father bought
   For two pieces of money:

   > A kid, a kid.

5. Then came *the fire*, and burned the staff
   That beat the dog,
   That bit the cat,
   That ate the kid,
   That my father bought
   For two pieces of money:

   > A kid, a kid.

6. Then came *the water*, and quenched the fire,
That burned the staff,
That beat the dog,
That bit the cat,
That ate the kid,
That my father bought
For two pieces of money:
                    A kid, a kid.

7. Then came *the ox* and drank the water,
That quenched the fire,
That burned the staff,
That beat the dog,
That bit the cat,
That ate the kid,
That my father bought
For two pieces of money:
                    A kid, a kid.

8. Then came *the butcher*, and slew the ox,
That drank the water,
That quenched the fire,
That burned the staff,
That beat the dog,
That bit the cat,
That ate the kid,
That my father bought
For two pieces of money:
                    A kid, a kid.

9. Then came *the angel of death*, and killed the butcher,
That slew the ox,
That drank the water,
The quenched the fire,
That burned the staff,
That beat the dog,

That bit the cat,
That ate the kid,
That my father bought
For two pieces of money:

A kid, a kid.

10. Then came *the Holy One*, blessed be He
And killed the angel of death,
That killed the butcher,
That slew the ox,
That drank the water,
That quenched the fire,
That burned the staff,
That beat the dog,
That bit the cat,
That ate the kid,
That my father bought
For two pieces of money:

A kid, a kid.

The following is the interpretation:

1. The kid, which was one of the pure animals, denotes the Hebrews. The father by whom it was purchased is Jehovah, who represents Himself as sustaining this relation to the Hebrew nation. The two pieces of money signify Moses and Aaron, through whose mediation the Hebrews were brought out of Egypt.

2. The cat denotes the Assyrians, by whom the ten tribes were carried into captivity.

3. The dog is symbolical of the Babylonians.

4. The staff signifies the Persians.

5. The fire indicates the Grecian empire under Alexander the Great.

6. The water betokens the Roman, or the fourth of the great monarchies to whose dominion the Jews were subjected.

7. The ox is a symbol of the Saracens, who subdued Palestine, and brought it under the caliphate.

8. The butcher that killed the ox denotes the crusaders, by whom the Holy Land was wrested out of the hands of the Saracens.

9. The angel of death signifies the Turkish power, by which the land of Palestine was taken from the Franks, and to which it is still subject.

10. The commencement of the tenth stanza is designed to show that God will take signal vengeance on the Turks, immediately after whose overthrow the Jews are to be restored to their own land, and live under the government of their long-expected Messiah.

An old woman was sweeping her house, and she found a little crooked sixpence. "What," said she, "shall I do with this little sixpence? I will go to market and buy a little pig." As she was coming home she came to a stile; the piggy would not go over the stile.

She went a little farther, and she met a dog. So she said to the dog, "Dog! bite pig; piggy won't go over the stile, and I shan't get home to-night." But the dog would not.

She went a little farther, and she met a stick. So she said, "Stick! stick! beat dog; dog won't bite pig; piggy won't get over the stile, and I shan't get home to-night." But the stick would not.

She went a little farther, and she met a fire. So she said, "Fire! fire! burn stick; stick won't beat dog; dog won't bite pig," (*and so forth, always repeating the foregoing words.*) But the fire would not.

She went a little farther, and she met some water. So she said, "Water! water! quench fire; fire won't burn stick," &c. But the water would not.

She went a little farther, and she met an ox. So she said, "Ox! ox! drink water; water won't quench fire," &c. But the ox would not.

She went a little farther, and she met a butcher. So she said, "Butcher! butcher! kill ox; ox won't drink water," &c. But the butcher would not.

She went a little farther, and she met a rope. So she said, "Rope! rope! hang butcher; butcher won't kill ox," &c. But the rope would not.

So she went a little farther, and she met a rat. So she said, "Rat! rat! gnaw rope; rope won't hang butcher," &c. But the rat would not.

So she went a little farther, and she met a cat. So she said, "Cat! cat! kill rat, rat won't gnaw rope,"

&c. But the cat said to her, "If you will go to yonder cow and fetch me a saucer of milk, I will kill the rat." So away went the old woman to the cow.

But the cow said to her, "If you will go to yonder haystack* and fetch me a handful of hay, I'll give you the milk." So away went the old woman to the haystack; and she brought the hay to the cow.

As soon as the cow had eaten the hay she gave the old woman the milk, and away she went with it in a saucer to the cat.

As soon as the cat had lapped up the milk, the cat began to kill the rat; the rat began to gnaw the rope; the rope began to hang the butcher; the butcher began to kill the ox; the ox began to drink the water; the water began to quench the fire; the fire began to burn the stick; the stick began to beat the dog; the dog began to bite the pig; the little pig in a fright jumped over the stile; and so the old woman got home that night.

* Or haymakers, proceeding thus in the stead of the rest of this paragraph: "And fetch me a wisp of hay, I'll give you the milk." So away the old woman went; but the haymakers said to her, "If you will go to yonder stream and fetch us a bucket of water, we'll give you the hay." So away the old woman went, but when she got to the stream, she found the bucket was full of holes. So she covered the bottom with pebbles, and then filled the bucket with water, and away she went back with it to the haymakers, and they gave her a wisp of hay.

Titty Mouse and Tatty Mouse both lived in a house,
Titty Mouse went a-leasing, and Tatty Mouse went
   a-leasing
  So they both went a-leasing.

Titty Mouse leased an ear of corn, and Tatty Mouse
   leased an ear of corn,
  So they both leased an ear of corn.

Titty Mouse made a pudding, and Tatty Mouse made a
   pudding,
  So they both made a pudding.

And Tatty Mouse put her pudding into the pot to boil,
But when Titty went to put hers in the pot, it tumbled
   over and scalded her to death.

Then Tatty sat down and wept. Then a three-legged stool said, "Tatty, why do you weep?" "Titty's dead," said Tatty, "and so I weep." Then said the stool, "I'll hop;" so the stool hopped. Then a besom in the corner of the room said, "Stool, why do you hop?" "Oh!" said the stool, "Titty's dead, and Tatty weeps, and so I hop." Then said the besom, "I'll sweep;" so the besom began to sweep. Then said the door, "Besom, why do you sweep?" "Oh!" said the besom, "Titty's dead, and Tatty weeps, and the stool hops, and so I sweep." Then said the door, "I'll jar;" so the door jarred. Then said the window, "Door, why do you jar?" "Oh!" said the door, "Titty's dead, and Tatty weeps, and the stool hops, and the besom sweeps, and so I jar." Then said the window, "I'll creak;" so the window creaked. Now, there was an old form outside the house, and when the window creaked, the form said, "Window, why do you creak?" "Oh!" said the window, "Titty's dead, and Tatty weeps, and the stool hops, and the besom sweeps, the door jars, and so I creak." Then said the old form, "I'll run round the house;" then the old form ran round the house. Now, there was a fine large walnut-tree growing by the cottage, and the tree said to the form, "Form, why do you run round the house?" "Oh!" said the form, "Titty's dead, and Tatty weeps, and the stool hops, and the besom sweeps, the door jars, and the window creaks, and so I run round the house." Then said the walnut tree, "I'll shed my leaves;" so the walnut-tree shed all its beautiful green leaves. Now, there was a little bird perched on one of the boughs of the tree, and when all the leaves fell, it said, "Walnut-tree, why do you shed your leaves?" "Oh!" said the tree, "Titty's dead, and Tatty weeps, the stool hops, and the besom sweeps, the door jars, and the window creaks, the old form runs round the house, and so I shed my leaves." Then said the little bird, "I'll moult all my feathers;" so he moulted all his pretty feathers. Now, there was a little girl walking below, carrying a jug of milk for her brothers' and sisters' supper, and when she saw the poor little bird moult all its feathers, she said, "Little bird, why do you moult all your feathers?" "Oh!" said the little bird, "Titty's dead, and Tatty weeps, the stool hops, and the besom sweeps, the door jars, and the window creaks, the old form runs round the house, the walnut-tree sheds its leaves, and so I moult all my feathers." Then said the little girl, "I'll spill the milk;" so she dropped the pitcher and spilt the milk. Now, there was an old man just by on the top of a ladder thatching a rick, and when he saw the little girl spill the milk, he said, "Little girl, what do you mean by spilling the milk? Your little brothers and sisters must go without their supper." Then said the little girl, "Titty's dead, and Tatty weeps, the stool hops, and the besom sweeps, the door jars, and the window creaks, the the old form runs round the house, the walnut-tree sheds all its leaves, the little bird moults all its feathers, and so I spilt the milk." "Oh!" said the old man, "then I'll tumble off the ladder and break my neck;" so he tumbled off the ladder and broke his neck. And when the old man broke his neck, the great walnut-tree fell down with a crash, and upset the old form and house, and the house falling knocked the window out, and the window knocked the door down, and the door upset the besom, the besom upset the stool, and poor little Tatty Mouse was buried beneath the ruins.

Fireside Stories.

THE STORY OF THE THREE LITTLE PIGS.

ONCE upon a time there was an old sow with three little pigs, and as she had not enough to keep them, she sent them out to seek their fortune. The first that went off met a man with a bundle of straw, and said to him, "Please, man, give me that straw to build me a house;" which the man did, and the little pig built a house with it. Presently came along a wolf, and knocked at the door and said, "Little pig, little pig, let me come in."

To which the pig answered, "No, no, by the hair of my chiny chin chin."

The wolf then answered to that, "Then I'll huff, and I'll puff, and I'll blow your house in." So he huffed, and he puffed, and he blew his house in, and ate up the little pig.

The second little pig met a man with a bundle of furze, and said, "Please, man, give me that furze to build a house;" which the man did, and the pig built his house. Then along came the wolf, and said, "Little pig, little pig, let me come in."

"No, no, by the hair of my chiny chin chin."

"Then I'll puff, and I'll huff, and I'll blow your house in." So he huffed, and he puffed, and he puffed, and he huffed, and at last he blew the house down, and he ate up the little pig.

The third little pig met a man with a load of bricks, and said, "Please, man, give me those bricks to build a house with;" so the man gave him the bricks, and he built his house with them. So the wolf came, as he did to the other little pigs, and said, "Little pig, little pig, let me come in."

"No, no, by the hair of my chiny chin chin."

"Then I'll huff, and I'll puff, and I'll blow your house in."

Well, he huffed, and he puffed, and he huffed, and he puffed, and he puffed, and he huffed; but he could *not* get the house down. When he found that he could not, with all his huffing and puffing, blow the house down, he said, "Little pig, I know where there is a nice field of turnips."

"Where?" said the little pig.

"Oh, in Mr. Smith's home-field, and if you will be ready to-morrow morning I will call for you, and we will go together, and get some for dinner."

"Very well," said the little pig, "I will be ready. What time do you mean to go?"

"Oh, at six o'clock."

Well, the little pig got up at five, and got the turnips before the wolf came—(which he did about six)—and who said, "Little pig, are you ready?"

The little pig said, "Ready! I have been, and come back again, and got a nice pot-full for dinner."

The wolf felt very angry at this, but thought that he would be *up to* the little pig somehow or other, so he he said, "Little pig, I know where there is a nice apple-tree."

"Where?" said the pig.

"Down at Merry-garden," replied the wolf, "and if you will not deceive me I will come for you, at five o'clock to-morrow, and we will go together and get some apples."

Well, the little pig bustled up the next morning at four o'clock, and went off for the apples, hoping to get back before the wolf came; but he had farther to go, and had to climb the tree, so that just as he was coming down from it, he saw the wolf coming, which, as you may suppose, frightened him very much. When the wolf came up he said, "Little pig, what! are you here before me? Are they nice apples?"

"Yes, very," said the little pig. "I will throw you down one;" and he threw it so far, that, while the wolf was gone to pick it up, the little pig jumped down and ran home.

The next day the wolf came again, and said to the little pig, "Little pig, there is a fair at Shanklin this afternoon, will you go?"

"Oh, yes," said the pig, "I will go; what time shall you be ready?"

"At three," said the wolf.

So the little pig went off before the time as usual, and got to the fair, and bought a butter-churn, which he was going home with, when he saw the wolf coming. Then he could not tell what to do. So he got into the churn to hide, and by so doing turned it round, and it rolled down the hill with the pig in it, which frightened the wolf so much, that he ran home without going to the fair. He went to the little pig's house, and told him how frightened he had been by a great round thing which came down the hill past him. Then the little pig said, "Hah, I frightened you, then? I had been to the fair and bought a butter-churn, and when I saw you, I got into it, and rolled down the hill." Then the wolf was very angry indeed, and delared he *would* eat up the little pig, and that he would get down the chimney after him. When the little pig saw what he was about, he hung on the pot full of water, and made up a blazing fire, and, just as the wolf was coming down, took off the cover, and in fell the wolf; so the little pig put on the cover again in an instant, boiled him up, and ate him for supper, and lived happy ever after.

TEENY-TINY.[*]

ONCE upon a time there was a teeny-tiny woman lived in a teeny-tiny house in a teeny-tiny village. Now, one day this teeny-tiny woman put on her teeny-tiny bonnet, and went out of her teeny-tiny house to take a teeny-tiny walk. And when this teeny-tiny woman had gone a teeny-tiny way, she came to a teeny-tiny gate; so the teeny-tiny woman opened the teeny-tiny gate, and went into a teeny-tiny churchyard. And when this teeny-tiny woman had got into the teeny-tiny churchyard, she saw a teeny-tiny bone on a teeny-tiny grave, and the teeny-tiny woman said to her teeny-tiny self, "This teeny-tiny bone will make me some teeny-tiny soup for my teeny tiny supper " So the teeny-tiny

---

[*]This simple tale seldom fails to rivet the attention of children, especially if well told. The last two words should be said loudly with a start. It was obtained from oral tradition.

woman put the teeny-tiny bone into her teeny-tiny pocket, and went home to her teeny-tiny house.

Now when the teeny-tiny woman got home to her teeny-tiny house, she was a teeny-tiny tired; so she went up her teeny-tiny stairs to her teeny-tiny bed, and put the teeny-tiny bone into a teeny-tiny cupboard. And when this teeny-tiny woman had been asleep a teeny-tiny time, she was awakened by a teeny-tiny voice from the teeny-tiny cupboard, which said, "Give me my bone!" And this teeny-tiny woman was a teeny-tiny frightened, so she hid her teeny-tiny head under the teeny-tiny clothes, and went to sleep again. And when she had been to sleep again a teeny-tiny time, the teeny-tiny voice again cried out from the teeny-tiny cupboard a teeny-tiny louder, "*Give me my bone!*" This made the teeny-tiny woman a teeny-tiny more frightened, so she hid her teeny-tiny head a teeny-tiny farther under the teeny-tiny clothes. And when the teeny-tiny woman had been to sleep again a teeny-tiny time, the teeny-tiny voice from the teeny-tiny cupboard said again a teeny-tiny louder, "GIVE ME MY BONE!" At this the teeny-tiny woman was a teeny-tiny bit more frightened, but she put her teeny-tiny head out of the teeny-tiny clothes, and said in her loudest teeny-tiny voice, "TAKE IT!!"

THE MISER AND HIS WIFE.*

ONCE upon a time there was an old miser, who lived with his wife near a great town, and used to put by every bit of money he could lay his hands on. His wife was a simple woman, and they lived together without quarreling, but she was obliged to put up with very

---

* "Let us cast away nothing," says Mr. Gifford, "for we know not what use we may have for it." So will every one admit whose reading has been sufficiently extensive to enable him to judge of the value of the simplest traditional tales. The present illustrates a passage in Ben Jonson in a very remarkable manner:

> —Say we are robbed,
> If any come to borrow a spoon or so;
> I will not have Good Fortune or God's Blessing
> Let in while I am busy.

hard fare. Now, sometimes, when there was a sixpence she thought might be spared for a comfortable dinner or supper, she used to ask the miser for it, but he would say, "No, wife, it must be put by for Good Fortune." It was the same with every penny he could get hold of, and, notwithstanding all she could say, almost every coin that came into the house was "put by for Good Fortune."

The miser said this so often that some of his neighbors heard him, and one of them thought of a trick by which he might get the money. So the first day that the old chuff was away from home, he dressed himself like a wayfaring man, and knocked at the door. "Who are you?" said the wife. He answered, "I am Good Fortune, and I am come for the money which your husband has laid by for me." So this simple woman, not suspecting any trickery, readily gave it to him, and when her good man came home, told him very pleasantly that Good Fortune had called for the money which had been kept so long for him.

THE THREE QUESTIONS.

THERE lived formerly in the county of Cumberland a nobleman who had three sons, two of whom were comely and clever youths, but the other was a natural fool, named Jack, who was generally dressed in a parti-colored coat and a steeple-crowned hat with a tassel, as became his condition. Now, the King of the East Angles had a beautiful daughter, who was distinguished by her great ingenuity and wit, and he issued a decree that whoever should answer three questions put to him by the Princess should have her in marriage, and be heir to the crown at his decease. Shortly after this decree was published, news of it reached the ears of the nobleman's sons, and the two clever ones determined to have a trial, but they were sadly at a loss to prevent their idiot brother from going with them. They could not by any means get rid of him, and were compelled at length to let Jack accompany them. They had not gone far before Jack shrieked with laughter, saying, "I have found an egg." "Put it in your pocket," said the brothers. A little while afterwards he burst out into another fit of laughter on finding a crooked hazel stick, which he also put in his pocket; and a third time he again laughed extravagantly because he found a nut. That also was put with his other treasures.

When they arrived at the palace, they were immediately admitted on mentioning the nature of their business, and were ushered into a room where the Princess and her suite were sitting. Jack, who never stood on ceremony, bawled out, "What a troop of fair ladies we've got here!" "Yes," said the Princess, "we are fair ladies, for we carry fire in our bosoms." "Do you?" said Jack, "then roast me an egg," pulling out the egg from his pocket. "How will you get it out again?" said the Princess. "With a crooked stick," replied Jack, producing the hazel. "Where did that come from?" said the Princess. "From a nut," answered Jack, pulling out the nut from his pocket. And "thus the fool of the family," having been the first to answer the questions of the Princess, was married to her the next day, and ultimately succeeded to the throne.

THE CAT AND THE MOUSE.*

The cat and the mouse
Played in the malt-house:

The cat bit the mouse's tail off. "Pray, puss, give me my tail." "No," says the cat, "I'll not give you your tail, till you go to the cow, and fetch me some milk."

First she leapt, and then she ran,
Till she came to the cow, and thus began,—

"Pray, cow, give me milk, that I may give cat milk, that cat may give me my own tail again." "No," said the cow, "I will give you no milk, till you go to the farmer and get me some hay."

First she leapt, and then she ran,
Till she came to the farmer, and thus began,—

*This tale has been traced back fifty years, but it is probably considerably older.

"Pray, farmer, give me hay, that I may give cow hay, that cow may give me milk, that I may give cat milk, that cat may give me my own tail again." "No," says the farmer, "I'll give you no hay, till you go to the butcher and fetch me some meat."

First she leapt, and then she ran,
Till she came to the butcher, and thus began,—

Pray, butcher, give me meat, that I may give farmer meat, that farmer may give me hay, that I may give cow hay, that cow may give me milk, that I may give cat milk, that cat may give me my own tail again." "No," says the butcher, "I'll give you no meat till you go to the baker and fetch me some bread."

First she leapt, and then she ran,
Till she came to the baker, and thus began,—

"Pray, baker, give me bread, that I may give butcher bread, that butcher may give me meat, that I may give farmer meat, that farmer may give me hay, that I may give cow hay, that cow may give me milk, that I may give cat milk, that cat may give me my own tail again."

"Yes," says the baker, "I'll give you some bread,
But if you eat my meal, I'll cut off your head."

Then the baker gave mouse bread, and mouse gave butcher bread, and butcher gave mouse meat, and mouse gave farmer meat, and farmer gave mouse hay, and mouse gave cow hay, and cow gave mouse milk, and mouse gave cat milk, and cat gave mouse her own tail again!

INDEX.

FOURTH CLASS.
PROVERBS.

FIFTH CLASS.
SCHOLASTIC.

ELEVENTH CLASS.

PARADOXES.

TWELFTH CLASS.

LULLABIES.

THIRTEENTH CLASS.

JINGLES.

FOURTEENTH CLASS.

NATURAL HISTORY.

FIFTEENTH CLASS.

RELICS.

SIXTEENTH CLASS.

LOCAL.

SEVENTEENTH CLASS.

LOVE AND MATRIMONY.

EIGHTEENTH CLASS.

ACCUMULATIVE STORIES.

NINETEENTH CLASS.

FIRESIDE STORIES.

Printed in the United Kingdom by
Lightning Source UK Ltd., Milton Keynes
141475UK00001B/143/P